I THOUGHT
IT WAS A
SIGN

ALSO BY DAYNA MASON (REID)

By Dayna Mason

NONFICTION
Dayna's Dose: A Prescription of Articles to Enrich Your Life

Women Over 50: The A to Z of It

Magnanimous: Be The One Everyone Wants to Do Business With

I'm Just That Into Me: You Are Who You've Been Waiting For

CHILDREN
Mosley the Feelings Monster (a children's book)

By Dayna Reid

NONFICTION
Do-It-Yourself Wedding Ceremony: Choosing the Perfect Words and Officiating Your Unforgettable Day

Funerals & Memorials: Creating the Perfect Service to Remember a Loved One

Officiating Weddings: Start a Profitable Business Marrying Couples

Wedding Officiant Guidebook for Beginners: How to Become Ordained and Perform a Marriage Ceremony Script

I THOUGHT IT WAS A

Sign

A Novella

DAYNA MASON

Visit the author's website:

www.daynajo.com

Published by Seattle Indie Press

Seattle Indie Press
publishing

ISBN: 9780997893854

Cover design by Dayna Mason
Printed in the United States of America

Dedicated to:

All the beautiful humans in my life and out in the world who provide safe spaces for the people they love to grow into who they were always meant to be.

Contents

"Love doesn't reveal itself through your willingness to endure its absence. To endure without love is strength. But it is not love."
—Reid

"The soul doesn't require answers to begin again. Only space to breathe." —Reid

"Drift is not the loss of direction. It is the shedding of maps drawn by fear." -Reid

"When you stop managing the forecast, you remember you are the weather." -Reid

"To remain unseen may keep you safe, but it will also keep you from yourself." -Reid

"It's not failure to leave behind what never belonged to you." -Reid

I THOUGHT
IT WAS A
SIGN

Signs

"Symbols are powerful because they are the visible signs of invisible realities."

- St. Augustine

Synchronicity

"Synchronicity is a meaningful coincidence which appears between mental state and an event occurring in the external world."

- Carl G. Jung

Serendipity

"Looking for something, finding something else, and realizing that what you've found is more suited to your needs than what you thought you were looking for."

- Lawrence Block

1

The Departure

"Love doesn't reveal itself through your willingness to endure its absence. To endure without love is strength. But it is not love."

—Reid

I THOUGHT THE trip I planned down to the last romantic detail would be the reset we needed, but he's on it—with *her*. Perfect way to say 'I love you': romance another woman.

"She was just someone to fill the seat," he said. "You were mad. I figured you wouldn't want to go." I'd been mad, yes. About his latest disappearing act, the flirty messages I wasn't supposed to see, the way he twisted things until I doubted my gut. But I never said I didn't want to go. I just wanted an apology.

Instead, he took the trip. With her.

He's probably sprawled out on the king-size bed I booked for *us*, sipping the wine I picked out for our arrival, next to the woman he once called "baby" but now swears is "just a friend." Platonic, he said, as if the word were a get-out-of-betrayal-free card, casting me as the jealous girlfriend who overreacts.

The real cruelty wasn't that he invited her; it was that he wanted me to bless it. To wait, like a fool, for his return. He called me from the train on his way to her, as if nothing had happened. "I love you, Anelie," he said. "You know we're meant to be. Forever, remember?" Sure, forever, with the occasional week away with another woman. I staggered between wanting to scream and throw up. As if someone stabbed me and was insisting it was fine. "I'll see you when I get back," he said, like we were between episodes of something that hadn't already ended.

I was gutted. This wasn't heartbreak. It was demolition.

When we hung up, I stood in the kitchen, staring out the window where we toasted sunsets with the Veuve Clicquot we brought back from France, certain we were building a life together. I searched for something, anything, to convince myself this wasn't happening.

That was two days ago.

I cried all my tears that first night, when I saw the photo she posted, his arm around her waist, her caption: *So grateful for old friends and new memories.*

There's nothing left to save. Nothing to return to. Whatever road we were on, he set fire to it and walked away smiling. What's left isn't tears. It's ash.

I've been smart with money. Saved, planned, bought my freedom. Retired early, and proud of it. I'm fifty-four with silver streaks in my brown hair (can't decide if it wants to curl or frizz, so I let it be). I live in leggings because anything that binds feels like a lie. I've never worn makeup. It clings like it's pretending to belong there. People tell me I look young for my age, like they can't believe I'm old enough to be retired, but that's also because I've learned to fake happiness well enough to fool even myself. I thought I'd spend retirement writing, that this would be my second act. A book, maybe more. But living someone else's life leaves no time for your own.

The two suitcases by the door are all I have to show for it. No home, no kids, and a life I shrank to fit someone else's. The rest is gone—the books, the dishes, the vintage writing desk I gave away because there was no room for it in his life. I thought this time would be different. I gave everything, believing it would be enough to soften him, to show him what love could look like. And he—charming, evasive, magnetic—took until there was nothing left.

I stand in the dimly lit, deeply male living room, all walnut tones and dark leather, the air thick with dust and day-old whiskey. The heaviness is suffocating. Brightness and light have always been my oxygen, but there was never room for me here. Not even in the air. The pool table swallows the room, a shrine to ego and unopened mail. I'd asked him to let it go, to make room for us. He refused, even though it hadn't been used in a decade. So we lounged in the cramped kitchen on rigid dining chairs, dwarfed beneath a bar-height table meant more for cocktails than connection. My hand rests on the back of one of the eight barstools no one ever sits on.

This was never *our* home; it's more like a dive bar that forgot to open. I just rearranged myself inside it.

I barely lift my feet as I move through the house, doing one last pass. The silk rose, now dusty, is still in the jar I put it in three years ago. My favorite flowers are carnations, not that it mattered. He tossed me the rose when he got in the car on the only Valentine's Day he ever acknowledged, saying, "Here. Happy Valentine's Day." Later, after a few too many whiskeys, he grinned that they were giving them out at the bar before he picked me up. When I didn't laugh, he said, "Oh, come on. That was funny." Not because it wasn't true, but because it was a joke to him.

Why did I stay? I sink into the one piece of comfortable furniture he let me talk him into buying, a small faux-suede armchair tucked into a nook by the kitchen. Out of the way, like me. At five-foot-one, my feet don't touch the floor. I run a finger over my lips, a familiar comfort I don't remember learning.

The signs were there. They always are. He warned me early on he had a wild past. Said he used to be a "player," but was "tired of the drama of chasing high-maintenance" women. I took it as honesty. Growth. Then came the charm: "If I were lucky enough to be with you, I'd never do anything to jeopardize that." And finally, the cliché that should've sent me running:

"You make me want to be a better man." Why did I hear that and feel chosen instead of warned?

He flirted with our server on our third date, complimenting her necklace, holding her gaze a little too long. "I'm just friendly. You're too sensitive," he said, as if that explained it. I laughed it off. Maybe I was. Then came the dodged questions, the way he made me feel needy for wanting what he'd promised. And still, I stayed. I saw potential. I believed we were both at a turning point. I've always been too good at loving the broken parts of people, just never learned how to stop doing it at my own expense.

My phone buzzes. A message from Michael.

Just checking in. How's the writing going?

I haven't heard from him in months.

A year ago, I messaged him after reading *Song of Wine*, his book on how choosing wine is like choosing music, personal. His words felt like an invitation to pull up a chair. He told me later he almost didn't reply, figuring a pretty woman messaging him out of nowhere had to be a scam. After I shared an idea I had for a book about how nurturing grapes mirrors human development, he responded with curiosity. We traded messages for a few months. Then life got loud again.

I never wrote the book. Or any book. I'm a writer who doesn't write. A seeker who doesn't quite believe. A lover who loves everyone but herself.

My specialty: spot the red flag, look away, stay anyway.

Michael's message is waiting. I type: *Honestly? It's not. I've been going through something.*

His reply comes fast: *I'm sorry. If you need space, I have a guest room. It's quiet here in Mystic. No pressure. You're welcome to stay as long as you like.*

Who does that? Who offers their home to someone they've never met?

I'm no stranger to impulsive decisions, and this might be a bad one. But Michael has always been gentle—sharing writing ideas, wine suggestions, check-ins I didn't know I needed. Something in me softens. A *man*, giving me room to breathe. Yes, I barely know him, and that should matter. But I trust it a little more than I don't. I book the train to Connecticut before I can talk myself out of it.

There's no one to call. I never had kids, not because I didn't want them, but because the men I chose were too self-centered to imagine a life that wasn't only about them—let alone one with a child. So, here I am. I let all my friendships go quiet, while I was busy trying to be his everything. That's what I do, I dissolve into *their* life. And when the relationship ends, I look around and realize I've exiled myself from the people who would've told me to leave sooner.

My mother did the same thing. Not with men, but with alcohol. She never talked about what hurt her, she just drank it quieter. Some days, she could be next to me and completely unreachable. She used to say, "You have to be strong." I thought that meant being quiet. Not needing too much. Being whatever the moment required so nothing would break. I was a circus performer for her, a skittish child, doing tricks that would earn her fleeting affection or avoid the next storm.

So I learned to tiptoe. Not to need. Not to ask. Not to burden.

I'm not sure I know any other way to be, but I don't want to disappear anymore. I don't want love as a reward for being easy. I want someone to love me—all of me, without having to be a "good little girl."

I don't have a plan. But I can't stay here, where my heart learned to second-guess itself, where his scent still clings to the pillows and his lies echo in every room. I can't be here when he comes back with a tan and excuses.

On top of the pool table, the corner of a book peeks out from beneath a year's worth of junk mail. I open it. Inside is a yellow Post-it in my handwriting: *He doesn't love you. He never did. He only loved what you could do for him.*

I wrote it the last time I packed my bags. The time I almost left.

Is it a sign? Possibly. More like confirmation that it's not just over, it's been over for a long time.

Maybe that's why Michael's message feels like more than kindness. Not a sign exactly, but a whisper from the part of me that still believes there is something better out there for me.

I stand at the drafty exit from my old life. My fingers tighten around the handles of my suitcases; my back straightens. My first choice, made without concern for what anyone else thinks. The door clicks shut. I don't look back.

There's nothing left here but the ghost of who I tried to be. And she can stay here, with the lies we told ourselves.

I'm done with both.

2

Arrival in Mystic

*"The soul doesn't require answers to begin again.
Only space to breathe."*

                                                            —Reid

THE TRAIN SLOWS with a sigh. I exhale too. *Okay, here we go.*
As I step onto the platform, a sea-salty breeze brushes my face, a
little insistent, as if the town's leaning in to say, *Welcome, Stay a
while. Maybe forever. No pressure.*

I run a finger over my lips. This place feels like it's been
waiting for me, like it knew I was coming. Which is comforting
and a little eerie.

In the small crowd, a man holds a hand-painted sign:
Welcome, Anelie! Did Michael paint that? The brushed lettering
is neater than most handwriting, and there's a watercolor wine
glass next to it, worthy of at least the art wall in a coffeehouse.

Either he's really that generous, which seems unlikely, or it's a down payment on something he wants later. I'm not sure yet.

Michael's shorter than I expected. He looks harmless, like someone's grandpa who spent his life quoting philosophers over breakfast while making your favorite scrambled eggs exactly the way you like them. Round wire-framed glasses rest on his nose; his collared shirt and sweater vest, topped with a beret, somehow suit him.

His warmth meets me before his words. "You must be Anelie."

"That's me," I say, still unsure about him, but no longer searching for the nearest escape route.

"For you," he says, offering me the sign. My hand hesitates, and that old feeling rises: I haven't done anything to deserve this. Could he really be that kind? The trouble he went to. The gentleness in his voice. I will the tears to stay put.

"Thank you," I say, the words not nearly enough for what I feel.

He reaches for my suitcases, and before I can stop myself, I step in and wrap my arms around him. Grateful. His arms close around me like it's the most natural thing in the world. No weirdness, just comfort. My shoulders surrender, and for a moment, my skepticism dissolves.

"Welcome to Mystic," he says, like it's a promise. I want to believe this welcome is real, but part of me is still waiting for the fine print.

On the short drive, I give him the condensed version of what happened. Enough to explain why I packed up my life and left, but not enough to unravel in the passenger seat.

"Sounds like you've been trying to fit where you never really belonged," he says.

"And losing myself in the process."

"No need for that in Mystic. We like people as they are."

He doesn't reach for solutions, just lets me feel heard. Maybe that's what I've been craving more than answers.

"I needed to leave him," I say. "But I think I needed distance from me just as much as from him. The me who couldn't stop going back."

"You didn't need a reason to come, but I'm glad you trusted me with one," he says, glancing over. "No need to smile through the nonsense here."

I lean back, trying on the idea of not having to pretend.

Water glistens between buildings. The stillness of Mystic seems to be watching to see what I'll do next.

Michael gestures toward a storefront nestled between a bakery and a spa the size of a closet. "See that bookstore?"

"Yeah," I say, eyes fixed on the chalkboard out front.

Welcome.
You didn't make a wrong turn.
You're exactly where you're supposed to be.

I almost believe it. The message feels like the outstretched arms of a fluffy grandma, ready to hug me until my defenses give up. Michael's voice breaks in.

"That bookstore thinks I'm a big deal," he says.

I glance at him, half-smiling. "Because you're always there?"

"Nope. Because they sold both copies of my book."

I shake my head, amused. He grins, and it's so unguarded, so warm, my laugh slips out before I can stop it. For a second, the heaviness lifts.

We pull into the gravel drive. His home is a charming white Cape Cod with black shutters, nestled into the land, offering assurance: *You're safe here.* A small vineyard stretches across the front yard, and rows of vines sway in the breeze as if they're nodding *hello.*

"Front yard grapes," he says, following my gaze. "A little stubborn, like their caretaker. But they ripen on their own terms, which I respect."

I smile, "So basically, those grapes have stronger boundaries than me."

"Maybe. But grapes don't worry about being chosen, especially not by people who don't deserve them." He arches a brow, amused with himself.

"Okay, I'll give you that one," I say.

He leads me through the light-filled, remodeled kitchen first. Stainless steel and copper pans hang above the island, and the smell of rosemary and roasted garlic permeates the air.

"In case you're up before me," he says, gesturing toward the coffee maker. "Just press the button. I'm useless before caffeine."

I laugh. "Good to know."

Next is the wine cellar, cool, dim, and lined with bottles. He names a few as we pass.

"A Sancerre that doesn't care what you think of it."

"A Barolo that demands your full attention."

He pauses before one bottle, smiling. "And a Syrah I only open when someone's life needs a better plot twist."

I laugh, but the words stay with me. "I'm hoping for the Syrah," I say, surprised I said it out loud. His look says he heard the part I didn't say.

Upstairs, the floorboards creak under my feet. Michael steps aside at a doorway. A ceramic lamp casts warm light across a bed dressed in crisp linens, while a vase of lavender and bergamot does a decent job of smelling like serenity. A writing desk faces the vineyard, its surface bare except for a single folded notecard, like it's daring me to sit down and finally write something. On the bookcase, his own *Song of Wine* sits beside *The Little Prince*, and it clicks. The man who writes about savoring the wine you love, not the one that's rare, is also the kind who knows grown-ups are terrible at remembering what matters.

The room looks like a boutique bed-and-breakfast. Only here, there's no checkout time.

"It's yours for as long as you need," he says as if reading my thoughts. He sets my suitcases at the foot of the bed and nods toward the notecard on the desk. "There's the Wi-Fi info."

I step closer. Below the password, he's added:

You don't need to know the way. Given space to breathe, good wine and good people arrive where they're meant to be.

"Dinner's in thirty," he says, eyes soft with understanding. "Take your time."

Out the window, the vines glow in the late afternoon light, swaying like they're breathing with me. I sit on the edge of the bed, unsure whether to brace or ease into it, drained in ways that aren't just physical. I want to relax, but this kind of welcome still feels like a test I might fail.

It's more than beautiful here. It's prepared. Thoughtful. Meant for me. As if he considered what I might need, even if I don't know myself. And I don't know what to do with that. I'm still waiting for the generosity to ask for something in return. But it hasn't. Not yet. I glance down at the card. *You don't need to know the way... good people arrive where they're meant to be.* Most of my life, I've followed maps that weren't mine, waiting for someone else to tell me where I'm allowed to exist. Routes drawn by others. Stayed on paths that looked safe, even when they felt wrong. Told myself they'd lead somewhere I could belong. Here, the path feels like mine. Which is both a relief and a little frightening. I have no clear direction, only the sense that I might be where I'm supposed to be.

The smell of roasted chicken greets me as I reach the bottom of the stairs. Michael moves easily through the kitchen, carrying himself with the casual confidence of an off-duty chef. He tastes the sauce, pauses, then closes his eyes, like he's letting the flavor tell him a story. A moment later, he opens them and adjusts the heat. No rush, no shortcuts.

He looks up as I enter. "Perfect timing," he says, setting a pan on the stovetop. "Dinner's almost ready. You hungry?"

"Starving, actually."

"Good. Tonight's menu: comfort disguised as gourmet cuisine."

He plates lemon-rosemary chicken, roasted carrots, and what he calls "grown-up mashed potatoes," which look suspiciously like regular mashed potatoes but with extra butter and herbs.

We move into the dining room. A weathered farm table anchors the space, built for lingering. Along one wall, a tall oak hutch shows off rows of delicate wine glasses, shaped for every kind of pour. On the walls, coastal paintings mingle with whimsical wine prints. Nothing tries too hard; it just welcomes you.

"This is a Viognier," he says, handing me a long-stemmed glass. "Light and citrusy, pairs well with unlearning old patterns."

I raise an eyebrow. "Label or your life experience?"

He grins. "Bit of both."

Dinner conversation is easy. He asks about the train, about what books I've been reading lately. What books I've been writing lately—none. He shares a story about a wine tasting where someone compared a Pinot to their ex-husband: "high-maintenance and not always worth it."

I laugh, and my chest feels lighter.

"Ever been compared to a wine?" I ask.

He thinks for a second. "Once. Someone said I was like a well-aged Rioja, deep and reflective, maybe a little stubborn, but more interesting with time."

"Not bad."

"Could've been worse. They could've said Pinot Grigio, polite and totally forgettable."

His grin lingers as we drink, and my attention drifts to a photo on the hutch, him with a woman holding a child. She's beautiful, in an unselfconscious way. Her smile is wide and easy.

I nod toward the photo. "Who's that in the picture with you?"

"My daughter's mother," he says, not looking away, but not inviting more.

I want to ask, where is she now? What happened? But something in the way he says it tells me there's a story, and it's not a light one. The kind that still echoes. So I don't ask.

Instead, I nod. "It's a beautiful photo."

He smiles faintly. "It was a beautiful moment."

And as if by agreement, we let it rest, the silence holding weight and respect.

"You up for a movie?" he says. "I have a theme going this week: wine films and the bottles that pair with them. Tonight's pick is *Bottle Shock.* A story about a wine that surprises everyone after it's had a chance to rest."

"Let me guess, the wine just needed the right environment to shine." I sense his choice wasn't accidental.

He lifts a bottle, a spark of amusement in his eyes, "This one's from Sonoma. Napa Valley Chardonnay, bright and underestimated, like the winemakers in the film."

He pours two glasses, hands me one, and clinks his glass lightly against mine. "To those who may surprise you once given room to breathe… and rosemary chicken."

I arch a brow, but it's all for show. The truth is, I feel seen, maybe even understood.

He nods toward the living room. "Shall we?"

He takes the recliner, leaving me the couch with a blanket draped across the back. No inching closer, no testing boundaries. Just presence. I ease into his kindness like borrowed warmth. *Could he really want nothing from me? Is that even possible?* I don't know. But I want to believe it is.

I watch more of the movie than I expect to, and when the credits roll, I realize I've forgotten to brace for anything.

"Some wines need time after travel," Michael says, as he takes a sip of his wine. "It's called bottle shock. Doesn't mean they're ruined. Just shaken."

I nod, holding my glass. "People too, I guess."

He tips his glass in a kind of toast.

"That was better than I expected," I say, adjusting the blanket over my legs.

He glances over. "You thought I'd pair a forgettable wine with a forgettable film?"

I smile. "No. I'm starting to see nothing you do is accidental."

His smile says I'm glad you noticed. We sit in the quiet. Not rushed to move. There's something unspoken in the air, comfortable, unassuming. The movie was about wine, but it drives deeper. Even the finest bottle can seem ruined when mishandled. But, with time and breath, it can become extraordinary. Maybe I'm not broken … just suffocating.

He sits forward. "I have to work tomorrow, early shift at the club. Should be back around six."

"Golf club?" I ask.

He nods. "I'm a wine steward. I pour overpriced Pinot for people who pretend they care about oak notes, when really they want the wine version of their favorite song."

"Fancy," I say, following him to the kitchen with our empty glasses.

"It keeps me in bottles and metaphors." He winks and nods toward the coffee maker. "By the way, I left a key to the house on the counter for you."

"So, what's the plan for tomorrow? Am I free to wander?"

"That's highly encouraged," he says. "Take your time. Drift, be curious. Mystic will handle the rest."

"You talk about Mystic like it's a person."

He shrugs. "Doesn't everyone?"

I narrow my eyes, amusement tugging at my mouth. "Should I be worried Mystic's planning an intervention?"

"Only if you ignore it." He smirks.

I give him a look, unsure whether to laugh or believe him. "Mystic sounds more invested in me than any of my exes. Low bar, but still." Honestly... I kind of hope it is.

He laughs, rinsing a glass. "Tomorrow night, Italian. And a movie about a man who tries to get rid of a vineyard, only to have it undo who he thought he was."

"An intervention sponsored by pours and pictures?"

He grins. "It's called *A Good Year*. Pairs well with Chianti and the moment you realize you're not going back."

I laugh. "Is that an omen?"

"Just a suggestion," he says, drying his hands. "I'm not here to fix you. Just feed you and casually pair dinner with your plot twist. Wine helps."

"Thank you." I pause. "For all of it."

"You're welcome. I know what it's like when your world cracks apart. Sometimes just having somewhere steady to land makes the difference between getting lost in it or finding your way through. Sleep well."

Holding his gaze, I let my smile say what my words can't, then turn toward the stairs.

"And Anelie?" he says, "Tomorrow, just breathe a little, see what shows up."

"Breathe. I think I remember how to do that."

"If not, Mystic will remind you."

I nod, the scent of a dinner that fed more than my body and the relief of not having to be anything but here, following me upstairs.

Through the guestroom window, the vineyard is barely visible in the moonlight. I switch on the little ceramic lamp and amber light softens the room. The quiet in this place doesn't just surround me, it holds me. The stillness is as attentive as the man who pairs wine with films and wounds with gentleness, who somehow understands that healing can't be rushed, only allowed.

My body loosens as it sinks between the cool sheets, still on alert but not bracing for the worst. The bed cradles me like it knows I've been strong for too long.

Outside, the wind moves through the vineyard, rustling the leaves in hushed waves. I close my eyes and listen. I'm not sure what tomorrow will bring. But for the first time, maybe ever...

I exhale.

3

The Drift

"Drift is not the loss of direction. It is the shedding of maps drawn by fear."

-Reid

FROM THE PORCH, fog blankets the vineyard rows and a cool, salt-tinged mist weaves between them like it has nowhere better to be.

I walk. No map, no plan, just the scuff of my well-worn Converse on the sidewalk and the low hum of Mystic waking up. The streets are Sunday-morning quiet, even though it's not Sunday. A few porch lights are still on, casting faint halos in the mist. A man in a wool cap sips coffee in a rocking chair, nodding like we're old friends. Wind chimes stir behind a fence. Overhead, a gull cries once, then vanishes. My welcome committee?

Everything feels slower here. Or is it just me?

Old seaside homes line the street, their paint peeling, their porches crowded with things someone loves. Nothing matches yet nothing feels neglected, as if perfection was never the point. This town makes flaws feel like stories, not failures. It seems to whisper, *Take your time. We're here for all of it.*

Guided by the part of me that still listens, I turn down a side street. A small brick-front shop with steamed-up windows awaits. Above the door, a sign trimmed in sea green reads:

Coffee Compass
Pointing you toward good coffee and better moments.

The door opens to a chime so subtle it feels like Mystic is saying, *She's here.*

The scent of fresh coffee and something buttery-sweet greets me. Exposed brick walls beneath wooden beams hold a collage of bookshelves and framed quotes; some wise, some silly. On the wall, a chalkboard titled *Reid's Reflection (to Question Direction)* contains a message, in crisp, almost architectural lettering:

What if knowing comes when we stop searching?
-Reid

The words catch me. I read them again. I'm not sure I've ever stopped searching long enough to let anything find me, least of all true knowing.

Another message by the register says: "Not all who wander are lost." - J.R.R. Tolkien

Someone's written underneath in blue pen: *Except me in the grocery store. Always me.* A laugh slips out before I have a say in it. From behind the counter, a barista peeks around a rack of mugs.

"Don't look at me," she says, already grinning. "I stand by it."

"Fair," I say, still smiling.

She steps into view, her curly purple hair piled in a messy crown. Her T-shirt reads ESPRESSO YOURSELF in bubble letters that sparkle under the lights.

"Ooh," she says, eyes widening. "You've got main character energy. I read energy and make scones."

"Hi, I'm Anelie," I say, caught between smiling and trying not to.

She leans in slightly, lowering her voice. "I'm Fia. You're gonna love it here. Mystic's weird in all the best ways."

A woman in her sixties approaches the counter, her silver hair pulled into a loose twist. Her black apron bears a stitched message: LOVE PEOPLE. SERVE COFFEE.

Her eyes meet mine, and her expression stills me, like she knows something about me I haven't said out loud.

"I'm Resa. You look like you got here on purpose, even if it wasn't your plan."

"That's a little cryptic… and oddly specific," I say, half-laughing, half-serious.

Fia rests her elbows on the counter. "Welcome to Mystic. We specialize in oddly specific."

Resa doesn't laugh, but her smile deepens, melting my defenses. "Don't worry, you don't have to have it all figured out to belong here."

"That's a relief," I say. "Because I definitely don't."

Fia slides a latte across the counter, bounces to the espresso machine, then pivots to the register like a human hummingbird.

Resa shakes her head and nudges a muffin her way. "You skipped breakfast again, didn't you? Sit. Eat."

Fia grins, guilty but unbothered. "Yes, Momma Resa."

Resa gives her a look that says, *I'll be checking.*

I order a coffee with cream, no sugar, and spot a table tucked in enough to keep to myself but with a view of the room.

I pull out my notebook. The page stares back, blank. I jot a line, cross it out. Nothing worth keeping. The words that usually spill out when I'm feeling this raw are silent. Like they've decided to sit this one out. The silence feels like proof that I'm not a writer. Maybe I never was.

Resa walks over carrying a small plate. "Scone," she says, setting it beside my coffee. "On the house. You look like you could use a little sweetness."

"Thank you." I'm caught off guard by the kindness.

She nods toward the empty chair. "Mind if I join you?"

I gesture for her to sit. "Not at all. I'm Anelie."

The cushioned bench gives slightly as I lean back, the window covered in fog. Between us is a single daisy in a narrow vase. Resa settles in with the ease of someone who's never felt pressured to fill silence.

Her gaze drifts to my notebook. "Writing," she says.

"Trying," I admit.

She nods, unsurprised. "I know that look, the stare-down between soul and page."

I laugh softly. "It's like everything I thought I had to say suddenly feels... small. Or stupid."

Resa tilts her head, studying me. "Maybe you're not trying to say something. Maybe you're trying to hear it."

The truth hits home. *I want to believe there's something meant for me to notice. Something to hear.* And yet...

"I don't know what I believe," I say, surprised to hear it out loud. "About signs, or guidance, or if any of it means anything. I guess I don't trust it anymore."

She doesn't flinch. Instead, she takes a sip from the mug she brought and studies me, like someone listening for more than the words.

"Did you used to believe?" she asks. "In anything greater?"

I almost say no. The safer answer. But the question settles between us like an invitation.

"Yeah. I did." My gaze drifts to the window. "When I was younger, before I started questioning everything, I believed something inside me knew the difference between right and wrong. Not rules. Something deeper. Something that knew what love would do... and wouldn't."

Resa nods, slow and steady.

"It wasn't about God the way people say. And it definitely wasn't about what people say is right. It was more like... an inner knowing. A compass inside me. And when I listened, things got clear."

I pause, then swallow. "But the world doesn't reward that kind of knowing, does it? We're taught to override it to be chosen. Taught to be good, follow the rules, fit in, to be wanted."

Her gaze remains steady.

"So I stopped trusting it. I let other people's wants get louder than my own voice." I glance out the window, then back at her. "But even now... the only guidance that's ever felt real came from love, not rules."

Resa studies me, slow and thoughtful. "If love's the compass, what's it pointing to right now?"

Hmm. What's it pointing to? I've always wanted love to stay. What I got was my mom, singing made-up songs one day and disappearing into silence the next. Once, she built me a Barbie house out of cardboard, wallpaper and carpet samples, even a tiny working door. It was magic. And then it wasn't. Her love showed up, then vanished like it had somewhere better to be. Maybe that's why I learned to take scraps as proof I was loved.

"I don't know," I say finally. "Maybe it's pointing to what's true, not what I want to be true."

She meets my eyes with a knowing smile and watches me, waiting for me to connect the dots.

I blink a few times. It tugs at a tender-ache; a longing for how it used to feel to believe.

"I haven't thought of this in years. When I was a kid, a pastor gave me a small plastic compass. I lost it in my twenties, somewhere between burying my mom and trying to find my value in a man's eyes. He called it a 'God compass.' I'd close my eyes and trust it knew where I was going, even when I didn't."

"Sounds like you've always known the way. You just quit trusting it."

Maybe she's right. The knowing I used to follow wasn't something I lost. Maybe I just stopped listening.

"I stopped trusting for a while, too, after I lost my boy." She reaches into her pocket. "I've carried this for a long time. I'd like you to have it." She places a small brass object between us. A compass, worn and beautiful, edges smooth, shaped by time and touch. An inscription is etched into the back:

There are no wrong turns.

I trace my fingers over the words. I can't explain it, but it feels like something behind the message is trying to get through. It's the same unsettled pull I felt when I first walked in, as if the town itself is holding its breath, waiting to see if I'll listen.

I turn it over. There's no needle. Almost a cruel joke; a compass to keep me lost.

"It's broken," I say.

Resa smiles, then winks. "Not broken. Just waiting on you."

Back at Michael's, the scent of roasted garlic lingers in the air, the Chianti breathing in my glass. Michael's dinner, yet again, has fed something deeper than appetite.

The compass is facedown beside my notebook, its brass back visible: *There are no wrong turns.* Not sure I believe that, but I'd like to.

Michael appears with the bottle. "More wine?"

I glance at my glass. "If I say yes, does that make me a wino?"

"Not until glass four. And even then, you'd still need a tragic backstory."

I lift an eyebrow. "Define tragic."

He grins, refilling my glass. "We'll call that a conversation for glass number four."

He takes a sip of his own, closing his eyes long enough to let it register. He drinks like it's an act of devotion, like there's no part of him anywhere else. I try not to stare.

The brass compass is cool in my palm. Holding it here, in this place where I can just *be*, steadies me.

We move to the living room, where I take my usual spot on the sofa. Michael queues up *A Good Year*. "Tonight's pairing: Chianti and not going back."

I laugh, but it snags on something raw. "Got a pairing for blocking your ex's number?"

"Definitely Chianti," he says. "Bold, unapologetic, and best enjoyed when you've finally decided not to settle."

"Here's to not settling," I say, raising my glass.

I swirl my wine to see what it feels like to appreciate something the way Michael does. Dark cherry and smoke rise to meet me. The sip is fruit and earth, bold and grounded. He's right, it's unapologetic. I hope I am, too.

The movie starts, all golden light and vineyards. The compass rests on the arm of the couch. No needle. No direction. No plan.

And somehow, I don't feel lost.

4

Becoming Weather

"When you stop managing the forecast, you remember you are the weather."

-Reid

THE GALLERY IS sunlit and spare, each painting placed with intention. Even the air feels curated. The stillness seeps into the space between my thoughts as I meander.

It's been over a week since I arrived in Mystic, and I think I'm starting to match its pace. I linger longer. Breathe deeper. Notice things I used to pass without seeing. Maybe it's the quiet. Or the way no one here expects anything from me. Or maybe I've finally run out of ways to distract myself.

A painting pulls me in. It isn't large, but it feels impossible to ignore. Swirls of deep blue, streaked with copper and soft white, arc across the canvas in layered movement. No clear shape. Just force. Like tidewater or wind.

The card below it reads:

Becoming Weather

*"She didn't leave because he changed. She left
because she could no longer be contained.
She was the weather—inevitable, wild—meant to
be experienced. Not managed."*

I blink against the blur that rises too fast to stop. There
were so many times I should've left. But I stayed. Not because I
didn't see who he was. But because I saw who he *could* be, if
someone just loved him well enough.

I poured love into every corner of his silence. Smoothed
over storms and made excuses for what he couldn't give.
Softened the edges of every hurt and called it understanding,
trying to be enough for both of us, until there was nothing left
of me.

He never said *shrink.* He didn't have to. It was in the way
he tensed when I cried. In "you're too sensitive," like my feelings
were the problem. In "the third degree" or "starting drama"
when I needed to talk. In how affection came only when I was
easy to love.

It wasn't cruelty. It was erosion. And I let it happen
because I wanted to be love. The kind that heals. That stays.
That lets someone be fully themselves—flaws and all—and still
feel safe. The kind that I longed for. Maybe that's what happens
when you've never had that kind of love; you try to get it by

being it. But love doesn't bargain. It doesn't fix. It just shows up. Or it doesn't.

This painting doesn't explain itself. It just *is*. Undeniable. My shoulders ease, something long-held letting go. The imperfect me isn't too much to love. Just too vast to contain.

A woman steps quietly beside me. Tall, elegant, a gray braid down her back.

"She painted that after leaving someone who told her she was too much," she says. "She told me, 'I wasn't too much. I was just too big for the box he needed me to fit in.'"

I turn to her, startled by her words. They echo the thought still warm in my chest, like she reached in and spoke it aloud.

I nod and turn back to the canvas. "That sounds... right."

She steps away, giving me space with it.

Near the entrance, a basket of postcard prints and a tin of pens sit beneath a sign: *Take something home. Let it remind you.* I find *Becoming Weather*.

Becoming. The word doesn't sit right. You can't become what you've always been.

For the painter, maybe it was becoming. For me, it's remembering.

I turn the postcard over and write: *No more proving I belong. I am the weather. I arrive.*

I tuck the card into my bag as a promise, a reminder, and I step into the daylight. A breeze carries salt and roasted coffee, warm and familiar. Across the street, the Coffee Compass sign swings gently. I don't even think about it. My feet already know where to go.

Fia spots me as I step inside. Her face lights up like she was hoping I'd walk in.

"Well, if it isn't our favorite wanderer." She pauses, then squints. "Okay, you're our only wanderer, but still. You've got a vibe."

I tilt my head. "Is that a good thing?"

"Please. You're giving *woman-in-transition-maybe-a-little-magical* vibes, like that moment in the movie right before everything changes, and she's just out there living her Tuesday, completely unaware the universe is about to go full soundtrack on her."

"I wouldn't mind a soundtrack," I say, half-smiling, letting the idea linger for a second. I glance at the board, where Reid's latest words are written:

When belonging is a cage, do you still belong?" -Reid

Reid has done it again. Tapped straight into my thoughts and chalked my latest insight, like he's tuned to the same frequency. He's right. Belonging that asks you to contain yourself isn't belonging. It's captivity. Maybe I didn't leave him. Maybe I left the cage.

Fia follows my gaze. "Right? I told Reid people can't be expected to wrestle with their identity before caffeine."

I smile. "Apparently, I'm the target audience for pre-coffee soul searching. His questions always feel like he's eavesdropping on my life."

Fia grins, "He's basically cosmic GPS. Reminds you where you are without all the annoying 'recalculating.'"

She pauses, the playfulness giving way to something heavier. "He used to teach philosophy, like, actual lecture halls and tweed jackets, I think. Then something happened. I heard it was a big heartbreak. Moved here maybe five years ago and just… stayed."

"That kind of loss changes you."

"It sure does," she says, as the lightness in her face slips for a second, like the shadow of her own pain breaking through.

"He's so kind, though," she says. "I'm convinced he was a golden retriever in a past life. He keeps an open tab here for folks who can't afford to pay. Doesn't want anyone to know it's him, told Resa to use it when someone looks like they need a reason to believe in people again."

She glances toward the chalkboard. "Seriously, he's like if Mister Rogers and a fortune cookie had a baby, only cuter."

I laugh.

"Okay," she says, clapping her hands once. "Are you ready for our beverage experiment of the day?"

I watch her like she's about to hand me a live frog.

She grins, undeterred, pulls out a mug and sets it down as if she's unveiling an enchantment. "Espresso, cinnamon, a dash of cayenne, and a splash of oat milk. I call it 'Third Eye Opener.'"

"Great, just what I need, an extra eye to over analyze everything."

"That's why I added the oat milk, to soften the revelations," she says.

I take a cautious sip. "Yikes, it's got a kick."

Fia nods, pleased. "That's the cayenne. It opens the third eye... or the sinuses. Either way, clarity."

I take another sip. It's surprisingly comforting. "I hate how much I like this."

She leans in. "You're welcome." She bows low, sweeps her arm like a magician revealing a rabbit, and glides toward the counter.

I can't help but adore her. She's completely wacky. And kind of wonderful.

I sit at my usual table and take another sip of Fia's metaphorical concoction. It does taste like discovery.

Outside, the fog is nearly gone, sun breaking through. I open my notebook and set the gallery postcard next to it.

Maybe becoming weather is about expansion. I write: *Love doesn't shrink. It expands. And it lets you expand with it.*

A voice rises from somewhere deeper. *You have to be strong.* My mom said that the day she sat on the edge of my bed in her faded floral muumuu, twisting a dishrag like it might wring out bravery. She'd just said the word "cancer." I was twelve. "We'll get through this," she said. "You have to be strong." So I was. Strong enough for both of us. For nine years. She died when I was twenty-one. A Monday in January. I waited for the world to pause. It didn't. Birds kept singing. People kept peopling. No one noticed except me. Her version of strong helped me survive. But it also taught me to stay silent when I needed to speak, to settle when I should've asked for more, and to endure what I should've walked away from.

I write: *Strength is telling the truth.* Underline it. Scratch it out. Try again: *Strength is walking away.* Cross that out too. Each version feels too small for what I mean.

Somewhere between crossing out lines and starting again, the conversations around me have shifted. New voices, same hum. Then, as if waiting for me to quit pushing, it arrives.

On a fresh line, I write: *Real strength is telling the truth, even when it scares you. And leaving, even when it breaks your heart.*

The espresso's gone cool in my cup. Outside, daylight has dimmed to dusk. Maybe that's what grief does—dims the world for a while, then lets the light back in slowly. I close the notebook. The page is mostly empty, but my mind isn't. Some things don't need ink to leave a mark.

As I stand to leave, Fia materializes beside me. "Wait." She holds up a finger like she's listening to an invisible radio. "Yep. Yep. Confirmed. You're coming."

"Coming to what?"

"Follow the Signs. This Friday. It's a town thing," she says. "Sort of like a scavenger hunt, but for your soul. With snacks."

She hands me a small lavender flyer that reads: *Follow the Signs. You never know where you'll end up—or what will find you.*

"I'll think about it," I say.

Fia winks, already satisfied. "Sure, think it over. The flyer's just for show, I already know you're coming."

I pause on the steps of Michael's home. The door is more of a threshold than an entrance—a crossing into a place where I don't have to be anything but here. Inside, Michael stands at the stove, sleeves rolled up, stirring something that makes my mouth water. "Welcome back," he says. "Tagliatelle with roasted garlic and wild mushrooms. I was about to open a Pinot."

I smile, setting my notebook on the counter. "Yum. Garlic, my favorite food group."

My phone buzzes. I check it without thinking. One line: *So that's it? No goodbye?*

It's him. He's back from his—no, *their*—trip. I wonder how long it took him to notice I was gone.

I stare at the screen. Dread drags me back to Day One, to the place where hope doesn't exist. Part of me wants to fire back. The nerve. As if I left for no reason. As if he hadn't been erasing me for months. But even the perfect words wouldn't change him into someone who could love me.

Michael stops stirring, concern flickering across his face. "Everything okay?"

I lock the phone without replying and try to keep my voice steady. "My ex just texted me. Said, 'That's it, no goodbye?'"

Michael turns slowly, wooden spoon still in hand. "Wow." He exhales. "Classic. That's not a question, that's bait." His jaw tightens like he's replaying something he'd rather forget. "Some people know exactly which buttons to push."

"Yeah."

He sets the spoon on a folded towel, considers me for a second, then snaps his fingers. "Hold on." He disappears down the stairs toward the wine cellar and returns with a different bottle. "Change of plans. Tonight calls for that Syrah. Bold, earthy, and a little wild." He sets it on the table with a small, knowing smile. "Because someone's life needs a better plot twist."

When he mentioned the Syrah that first night, I didn't expect to qualify for it so soon. "I think you're right."

He pours the wine, slow garnet ripples, trailing down the inside of the glasses. "To a better plot twist."

"To taking back the pen," I say, giving the air a small nod, like I just signed an invisible contract.

We eat in easy silence. I twirl the tagliatelle, strands glistening with garlic-infused oil. The roasted garlic mellow and sweet, the mushrooms tender with an earthy depth that settles low and satisfying. Each bite grounds me, as if infused by whatever magic he's coaxed from the pan. The Syrah meets it with weight and warmth.

"I saw a painting today," I say, easing the quiet aside as I finish the last bite. "And it hit me—maybe I've spent my life holding back. Thinking love meant giving everyone else space, even when it left none for me."

Michael nods. "Art does that sometimes. It expresses the things we haven't found words for yet."

He's right. There are so many ways art speaks to us—through paintings, novels, songs that wreck us for no logical reason. Maybe art doesn't just reflect life, maybe it hands our hearts back to us.

"That's what I'm trying to do in my new book, *Nine Holes*," he says. "Golf on the surface, but it's really about giving people the disciplines that shape happiness. Comes from years in hospitality. Being an innkeeper was never about beds. It was about tuning the senses—reminding people to taste, to notice, to appreciate what was right in front of them. I'm just writing it now through the walk of a golf course instead of wine."

"I'd read that. Even if I have to survive golf metaphors," I say, with a side-smile. He shakes his head with a laugh under his breath, and we carry our glasses into the living room, settling into our usual spots. He queues up *Under the Tuscan Sun*.

I glance sideways at him. "Heartbroken woman escapes to a charming town with good wine, finds community and clarity. Sounds familiar."

His smile tilts. "And here you are, right on cue."

"You say that like you've got a script in your pocket."

He grins and takes a sip. "Well, if Diane Lane starts telling her secrets to a man who speaks in wine pairings... I'll start checking for camera crews."

I smile and shake my head. On screen, sunlight spills across olive trees and crumbling tiles. I rub the side of my neck, trying to work out the knots. "I think my body forgot what rest feels like," I say. "My shoulders are basically cement."

His eyes warm. "My friend Deni runs a spa. You'd like her. She's... well, you'll see."

"Alright," I say, already trying to picture her.

5

The Mask of Brightness

"To remain unseen may keep you safe, but it will also keep you from yourself."

-Reid

BLESSED, STRESSED, AND *about to feel your best,* reads the hand-lettered sign on the spa counter. Lemon and eucalyptus drift through the air, carried by low music that eases you the instant you step inside.

"You must be Michael's friend." A woman emerges from the hallway, her voice rich with warmth and sunshine. She's barely taller than the counter but moves with a presence you couldn't miss if you tried. Dark curls piled in a messy bun, a tailored lab coat over a blush blouse, makeup flawless—except the lip liner, which looks like someone outlined her mouth and forgot to color it in.

"You're adorable," she says. "And those Converse? Stop. I'm obsessed. I love you already, total boss babe."

I laugh, a little unsure, but I think she means it. "Thank you," I say, offering my hand. "I'm Anelie."

"Deni," she says, waving off my hand and hugging me like we've known each other for years. "I'm Cuban, we don't do handshakes. Welcome to the sanctuary-slash-circus."

She gestures for me to follow her down a softly lit hallway. "I'll show you around."

"That's where tension headaches walk in and vacation plans walk out," she says, pointing as we pass. "That's where cellulite goes to cry. And over there? That's where wrinkles rethink their life choices." She winks.

I can't help but laugh. We stop at a doorway where soft music hums, the lights are low, and a massage table awaits in low light.

"Joy's got you," Deni tells me. "You'll come out not sure what day it is… in a good way."

She opens the door and gestures inside. "See ya on the other side."

Forty-five minutes later, I float back out, loose-limbed and hair mussed.

Deni appears, holding out a mug. "Turmeric ginger tea. Because tequila at noon is frowned upon."

She pauses mid-step, one hand catching the wall. Her face goes a shade paler.

"Whoa." She laughs, shaking her head, hand still braced. "Guess coffee and stress aren't the breakfast of champions."

I start to say something, but she waves it off and sets the tea down like nothing happened.

"Okay, so, how do you feel?" she asks. Her voice bounces, but the color hasn't fully returned to her cheeks.

"Are you okay?"

"Oh, I'm fine. Just need more than caffeine and three hours of sleep. Enough about me. How do you feel?"

I can't get the image of her bracing against the wall out of my head. Still, I let her steer the moment. I sink into a plush chair in the lounge, surrounded by artfully placed throw pillows. "I think I melted a little."

"Perfect," Deni says, settling across from me. "That's the goal. Melt, then walk out of here like you own the sidewalk."

"Your place here is beautiful," I say. "It feels like it knows what people need before they do."

Her fingers turn the small gold cross at her collarbone. "Oh, it's nothing fancy. My boyfriend calls it a wannabe spa, for people who don't know any better."

She laughs, quick and weightless, the kind you perfect from years of dodging hurt. "I just wanted people to leave feeling better, so I pieced it together best I could."

I want to tell her it's so much more, that intention and kindness live in every corner. But she's already moved on, checking her phone for messages. It buzzes before she can put it away. Her brow tightens as she answers—on speaker.

"Can I call you back? I'm with a client."

A man's voice fills the room, sharp and exasperated. "You're still there? Of course. God forbid you show up on time for once."

Deni keeps her smile in place, though it falters at the edges. "I said I'll be there. I'm just running a little late."

"Sure, keep playing spa fairy. Because without your mud masks, where would we be?"

"I'm almost done," she says, quickly tapping the screen to end the call.

She slides the phone away face down on the table. Her smile remains but she is clearly somewhere else.

My gaze drifts. Their conversation tugs at something familiar. The way he makes her work sound smaller than it is. The way she laughs too loud, then shrugs like it's nothing. I had been named *Columnist of the Year* by the city, and there was a big party for me. I'd reminded him the night before, told him how much it mattered to have him there. He didn't show until the event was nearly over, then spent the rest of the evening locked in conversation with one of my more attractive friends. He leaned in, turning his whiskey glass between his fingers, all ease and attention, while I hovered at the edge like an uninvited guest. Later, he shrugged. *"What's the big deal? It's not like you won an award that matters."*

That night, I didn't cry. I just felt small. Like maybe I didn't matter either.

After that, the column felt hollow, so I stopped writing it. Eventually, I stopped writing much of anything.

Deni has bounced back, her brightness breaking through my memory of that night.

"That man's gonna turn my hair gray before menopause does." She laughs. "But honestly, I don't blame him. I'm a mess. I can't keep track of anything unless I write it on my arm in Sharpie." She plucks a jar from the basket on the table. "Want a sugar scrub sample that smells like vacation and unrealistic expectations?"

I'm about to answer when the bell at the entrance chimes. A woman walks in pushing a stroller, looking sleep-deprived but hopeful.

"Hey you!" Deni says, springing up and wrapping the woman in an exuberant hug. "You here for a massage? Did the cat ever forgive you for bringing home a baby? And how's Ava's cough? You try that eucalyptus thing I mentioned?"

The woman laughs and rolls her eyes fondly, seeming to know exactly what kind of whirlwind she's walked into and is grateful to be seen. "No, I was walking by and just wanted to say hi. And yes—still hates the baby, cough's better, and the eucalyptus made the whole house smell like fancy soap."

"Win-win-win," Deni says, slipping a tiny lotion bottle into the stroller's cupholder and giving a wink. "For when you're two sips of coffee from falling apart—but, obviously, still cute."

They chat a moment more, and the woman leaves, visibly lighter than when she arrived.

Deni returns to her seat like nothing happened. "She's a great mom. Her confidence just missed the memo. She almost believes it, just needs some reminding… and maybe a nap."

I nod and lean back into the chair, letting the feeling settle. Being around Deni is like sitting in sunlight you didn't realize you'd been missing.

She offers a jar from the side table. "Here's the scrub, lavender and sugar. Take it. Everyone should leave here with the hope of exotic trips and a flat stomach."

I thank her and step outside, still smiling, the jar in one hand and her brightness echoing in my ears. The sun has climbed higher and the air smells of sidewalk heat. My limbs feel looser, but under my ribs something stays tight; maybe the part of me waiting for permission to matter. I press my hand to the pocket with the compass, its weight more comfort than direction.

The "Columnist of the Year" memory returns. How invisible I felt that night, when he couldn't be bothered to show up, and made me feel stupid for wanting it to matter.

Deni deserves better than a man who can't see how much light she brings into a room, how people stand taller after being around her.

Maybe I do too.

Coffee Compass comes into view like a lighthouse. It's nearly empty, so the vibe is quieter.

Fia's not here, but Resa is.

She looks up and smiles like she's been expecting me. "Back again," she says.

I nod. "Spa day."

Resa raises a brow. "Let me guess, Deni sent you home with a scrub and two compliments you're still trying to believe?"

I hold up the jar. "Lavender, sugar, and apparently I'm an adorable, boss-babe."

She laughs. "Sounds about right."

"Chamomile," she says, setting down a mug in front of me. "You look lighter, and I'm not talking about the spa."

I curl my fingers around the warmth of the cup. "Deni gives so much to everyone around her. Makes people feel seen. Like they matter. But when her boyfriend said something—mean, honestly—she smiled. Laughed it off. Said she was a mess, a lot to handle… like that made it okay."

Resa's gaze holds mine, "Tucking yourself away can feel safe, and self-blame is how we talk ourselves into staying there."

"I hadn't thought of it that way."

Her words brush against something tender. Unsure what to say, I do what I've always done when I need to make sense of things. I pull out my notebook and write a single line on the next blank page: *You don't have to disappear to be loved.*

When I look up, Resa is watching me, giving me space to arrive at something on my own.

"You know, people like Deni," she says, "they're often the ones who think love is something you have to earn. Usually, because early on someone convinced them they weren't enough as they were."

I know she's not only talking about Deni.

"Did you ever do that?" I ask. "Shrink?"

Her smile is soft and a little sad. "Oh, I didn't just shrink. I disappeared. For years."

She traces the rim of her cup with slow precision. "It took me a long time to learn that abandoning yourself to please other people doesn't make you good. It just makes you bitter."

She doesn't say more. And I don't push.

I nudge the empty mug away.

Resa touches my hand. "I'm always here, with a warm beverage, and a reminder that you don't have to contort yourself to belong."

I thank her and step back into the sunlight. I *do* feel lighter.

When I reach Michael's, I am greeted by that now-familiar calm, a calm that feels like it's been waiting for me all along. Still, there's an undercurrent to the day, an opening, waiting for me to walk through.

6

The Picture

"It's not failure to leave behind what never belonged to you."

-Reid

MICHAEL HAS ALREADY left for the golf club when I head downstairs. There's a note on the kitchen counter: *Back before lunch. Sourdough's fresh. Coffee's better with company.* I smile. That's just like Michael, the practical delivered with something to think about.

The coffee maker is set up for me. He has done this every day of the last two weeks I've been here. My ex brought me coffee in bed. Twice. It felt like worship. After that, nothing. No coffee, no effort. I realize now, he wasn't doing it because he cared. He was doing it to impress me. To seal the deal. That's why it only happened twice. After that, there was rarely even coffee in the house. I told myself it wasn't a big deal, but I secretly longed for him to do it again.

Standing in Michael's kitchen, I feel the difference. There's no performance, just consistent care that doesn't ask for applause.

I push the button on the coffee maker. The echo of coffee brewing fills the silence.

It shouldn't seem remarkable to be considered. But it does.

On the porch, dew clings to the vines. The chairs are cool, so I pull a throw across my lap. A gull settles on the vineyard fence, tilts its head, and looks directly at me, holding eye contact longer than makes sense.

Jonathan Livingston Seagull. I haven't thought about that book in years. I read it in high school, underlining sentences I didn't fully understand but somehow felt were meant for me. Something about freedom and belonging.

The gull doesn't move. Just stares.

Is this a sign?

I remember Jonathan wanting to soar, but his flock wanted him to conform.

Maybe freedom isn't escape. Maybe it's no longer trying to belong where you never did.

This place. These people. Deni's radiant energy, Resa's mysterious knowing, Fia's wild logic that somehow spirals into truth—even Mystic itself, eerily present. And Michael, his kindness offered without condition, seemingly the only way he knows how to be.

No one here needs me to disappear.

I sip my coffee. This morning isn't extraordinary, but maybe that's the point. Maybe peace doesn't arrive with a declaration. Maybe it just arrives, sits beside you, and doesn't ask for anything. I open my notebook, the same one I keep meaning to fill, and write: *Sometimes, the ones who say they love you only love how you make them feel.*

I stare at the words. They're not untrue, but they feel like something I would've posted in the past; vague enough to sound wise, guarded enough to hide what hurt.

My phone buzzes. It's him. No words, just a photo of that dinner under the string lights. I'm smiling like I mean it. He's leaning in, glass raised, no arm around me. Just before, he'd told the table I was "one of his harem." Everyone laughed, including me. I laughed because it was easier than admitting I felt invisible. Easier than being the woman who "can't take a joke." But I can see it now—the emptiness in my eyes, the smile that doesn't quite reach. I was already disappearing, and no one noticed. And now, he sends it. Like a love note.

That's the telling part. He sent it, thinking it was a good memory. My finger hovers over the screen. I want to answer, to feel that rush again, like it was in the beginning when he swore, I was "the best thing that ever happened to him." I want to be chosen. Maybe he's learned. Maybe this time is different? But it isn't. He never wanted me. He never even knew me.

I don't respond, but I don't delete it, either. He sent it to remind me of what we once had. All it reminds me of is how lonely it felt to love someone who never wanted me. I don't miss him. I miss the beginning, when I thought his attention meant love.

Maybe we were both performing.

✳

Michael returns just before noon.

"I brought lunch," he says, setting a brown paper bag on the counter. "Figured we'd let the day unfold from there."

Lunch is simple: sourdough still warm, tomato soup with a hint of basil, a wedge of soft cheese, and a bottle of red.

"It's called Unscripted," he says, pointing at the label. "Best opened when the plan's gone out the window."

"Unscripted," I repeat, studying the bottle. "Fitting."

"Yeah. No script. Just shows up as it is. Impressive, in a bottle. Even better in a person." He nods toward the porch. "Let's take lunch outside. Perfect day for a porch picnic."

We eat in easy rhythm. Michael tears off a piece of sourdough and dips it in his soup. "I think I taste truffle oil."

"I don't even know what truffle oil is," I say. "Sounds like soup trying to be fancy." I set my spoon down. "Speaking of trying to be something you're not, he sent a photo this morning. My ex."

"Ah." Michael tilts his head, listening.

"He said something awful right before it was taken. I felt invisible. And now he sends that picture like it's a good memory?" My voice rises, sharper than I intend. My chest is tight. It's all still too close.

Michael gives a slow nod, like he understands more than I said, and none of it scares him off.

I breathe out, slow, testing the air between us. "Every time I wanted to leave, I stayed. Thought I could love him into changing. Now, I just feel stupid, like I failed at something I should've walked away from years ago."

Michael sets his glass down and leans back in his chair. "When people come into the club, and they're beating themselves up over a poor decision, I tell them all the same thing." He meets my eyes, steady. "Begin again."

The air feels different after he says it.

"When they think they've ruined something or think it's too late start over, it never is. You don't have to do it all at once. Just take a breath and begin again. I'm weaving this idea into my new book."

"You're right," I say. "My mistakes don't have to mean there's no future."

Michael stands and gathers the dishes. "I've got a little club paperwork to finish but take your time." He glances toward my notebook and winks. "Maybe even do a little writing?"

He disappears inside the house, the door swinging closed with a soft clack behind him.

The vines ripple in the breeze, all growth and tangle, finding their way without needing to know how.

Begin again. But how? I thought the signs were pointing to a relationship where I could finally just be me. Loved, flaws and all. That's what we both said. But he never meant it. Where do I even start, when I've been following a map that was never mine? It belonged to someone else, someone I wanted to love me. I searched for proof that we were meant to be, but deep down, I knew I was leaving myself behind just to stay near him.

I don't know what's next, but I know what we had doesn't feel like home. Maybe that's enough to begin again.

The breeze stirs, flipping open my notebook. It lands on a blank page. I chuckle. *Okay, Mystic, I can take a hint.* I write: *Maybe the real signs aren't chalkboard messages or the gift of a compass. Maybe they're the little nudges that say, "This isn't it."*

I read what I've written twice. It doesn't sound like a caption. It sounds like me. So many times I've attempted to write. I'd catch a spark, mention it to someone, maybe share a paragraph, and if they didn't light up, I let it go. Stop, start, stop again. Much of what I've written has been shaped by what I thought would excite someone else, by what felt safe to say. This feels different. This time I'm writing for myself.

I close the notebook and breathe in the salt air.

7

Signs of a Beginning

"The soil of every beginning is the ending you finally allowed."

-Reid

RESA'S BEHIND THE counter, restocking sugar packets with deliberate care. She glances at the laptop under my arm and smiles, raising her brows.

"Good," she says, as if I've confirmed something for her.

I pause. "Good what?"

"Just… good." She nods toward the alcove. "Your table's waiting."

The table with the single daisy.

Coffee Compass has become a kind of sanctuary, a place that says: You don't have to try so hard here. Plus, the smell of sweet pastry and fresh espresso never gets old.

Reid's message waits on the chalkboard as I pass the counter:

What if the beginning isn't something to seek, but what finds us once we've lived through the ending?

-Reid

Half a laugh slips out. Strange how a few words on a chalkboard can feel like someone reaching through the silence to say, "I see you."

The cushion gives under me, the screen stares back, title: *Signs.* On the table, the daisy tilts toward me, like it's keeping me company.

Fia appears from nowhere like a caffeinated apparition. She squints at the screen. "*Signs?* Yep. It's official. Mystic has claimed you."

I laugh. "It's just a title. I'm not sure what it is yet."

Fia waves her hand like it was never up for debate. "Doesn't matter. Titles know things before we do."

She pulls a tiny notebook from her apron pocket— *Evidence* scrawled across the front in purple glitter pen, and scribbles something with dramatic flair. "Phone battery at 22%, receipt total $2.22, and now the word *Signs?* That *is* a sign. Cosmic breadcrumbs."

Phone says 73%. Receipt was closer to five bucks. Not sure what alternate reality Fia's operating in, but I nod at her glitter-bomb notebook. "You keep track of signs?"

She looks up like I've asked whether she breathes. "Of course. The universe talks all the time. People just forget how to listen." She tucks the notebook under her arm, leans in slightly. "Today, if you see a feather? Pay attention."

"Feather," I echo, not sure what she means.

She grins. "They usually show up when you're right where you're supposed to be."

"Really," I say, the word standing in for *Sure they do.*

"Mm-hmm." She nods. "Life weaves things together. Most people miss it because they want it all mapped out, turn-by-turn, no surprises. But life throws feathers, not blueprints."

She looks at me like I already know. Maybe part of me does, the part I don't usually trust.

She twirls, because of course she does, and drifts back to the counter, humming *Don't Stop Believin'* like it's sacred.

The cursor blinks, daring me. I type one line, then another:

Maybe signs were real. Or maybe some moments were just too perfectly timed to ignore. Maybe they weren't messages at all, just echoes of what she already knew.

The words come easy, like breath. The man who chose someone else and called it friendship. What it meant to her to be too much for the boxes she tried to fit into; to be vast and wild, squeezed into a life carved by someone else. How being allowed to exist could feel like love, and how silence, when it was safe, could wrap around her like arms.

Memory becomes meaning, meaning becomes truth. Less like writing and more like taking dictation from somewhere beyond my thoughts.

By the time I stop, the screen is crowded with fragments, insights, the outline of a story more honest than anything I've ever spoken. Scrolling back through the pages, I'm stunned by how much has spilled out and how easily it came.

A familiar voice cuts in.

"Hey, stranger, mind if I crash your solitude?"

Above the screen stands Deni, looking like a woman on a mission. A Big Gulp-size coffee in one hand, phone and keys in the other. The keychain dangles with the message: *Bless this mess.* She drops into the chair across from me and presses her fingers to her temples. "This headache's trying to kick me out of my own head. Guess food should've made the to-do list."

A response barely leaves my lips before she waves it away.

"It's fine. I'll grab something on the way to Bible study, or there's always cookies in the car—don't judge."

"You joke, but I hope you eat something real today."

She sets everything down like she's moving in. "I was gonna bring lunch but ran out of time and patience."

"Patience with what?"

She hesitates. "Eric, mostly. And my mouth. I say things before I think, Jesus knows." She shrugs. "My mom used to say, 'If you had half a brain, you'd know when to shut up.' Real Hallmark stuff."

"That's awful," I say, unsettled by how easily she shrugs it off.

Deni's laugh is quick, practiced. "Yeah, well. She had a point. Eric says, 'That's our Deni. Heart of gold, brain of a squirrel.' He's not wrong."

I know that laugh. It's not amusement, it's armor. Rehearsed. Protective. A shield against pain.

She rips a napkin in half and brushes the pieces aside. "Anyway, enough about my sitcom of a life. What are you working on?"

"It's called *Signs*," I say, eyes on the screen. "Might be a book, or maybe therapy. Hard to tell yet."

"Sounds mysterious."

"More like messy."

She nods. "Messy is my spiritual gift."

I smile. "You ever look for signs?"

"Constantly," she says, sipping her coffee. "Usually in the form of whether my concealer's cracking."

"I mean real ones."

"What do you mean by real?"

"I don't know… the kind that feel like they're trying to tell you something. Even if you can't explain it."

She shrugs. "I used to. Now I just assume if Jesus wants to get my attention, He'll trip me."

I laugh. "Subtle."

"He knows who He's dealing with. Like Eric says, squirrel brain." She taps her temple. "Seriously, though, I used to think God was trying to talk to me. Now I figure He's just up there shaking His head like, 'Forget it, she's hopeless.'"

I want to tell her she's wrong. She wouldn't believe me, so I don't.

"I mean, He's got patience," she adds. "But even Jesus has to tap out sometime."

She makes everyone feel like they matter, yet thinks she doesn't, and believes in a God who sounds a lot like her mother.

"You really think God gave up on you?" I say.

She lifts a brow. "You met me, right?"

"What if love isn't something to earn, what if it just... is?" I pause. "Even the Bible says God is love. Not 'God loves you as long as you get everything right.' Maybe real love doesn't need us to do anything."

Deni picks at the corner of her paper cup. "I always thought that was just a thing people said, like those throw pillows that say *blessed* while your life's on fire. But really, I've always felt like God's got me on probation—watching to see if I'm worth the trouble."

"God doesn't sound very loving," I say.

"I mean, I know Jesus loves me, I just think He's disappointed. Like, not mad—just tired."

"Tired of what?" I ask.

"Of me messing up. Picking the wrong guys. Saying I'll do better, then going back to the same old stupid stuff. That kind of thing."

"Love shouldn't feel like a test. With my ex I thought if I could just be better—more patient, less needy—he'd love me."

"And now?"

"I think maybe I've been trying to earn something that was never love to begin with. If love is real, it doesn't leave when you screw up. It doesn't need you to prove anything. It just… stays."

She shrugs, but it's more defense than indifference. "That sounds nice. But the only thing that ever stayed in my life was debt."

She leans back, studying me. "You sound like my old pastor, except with cuter shoes and less creepy."

I laugh, half flattered, half creeped out. "I'm not trying to preach."

"Good," she says, smirking. "I already tithe in lip liner."

She looks down at the lid of her coffee cup like something's written there. "So, you really think love is that easy. It just shows up, no strings?"

"I think so." My eyes drift back to the screen. "Maybe signs are little pointers to where love lives."

She squints at me like I'm speaking a foreign language.

"Or maybe I'm writing to figure that out," I say.

She holds my gaze a bit longer than usual, then nods like that's enough, and gathers her things. "Alright, enough deep thoughts. I've got a client coming in who wants her forehead to look 'less judgmental.'"

She pauses before leaving. "You *should* write a book. That's some Oprah-level stuff."

"Maybe I will."

"Jesus loves you," she says as she walks off. "Me, He's still rolling His eyes at."

The door swings shut behind her, the sound of her heels fading.

Back on the screen, *Signs*.

Maybe she's right.

The restaurant is tucked into the edge of the marina. Wooden beams, paper menus, wine by the glass, and servers who know when not to hover.

"This place has the best cioppino," Michael says as the server sets down the menus. "Makes you swear you're in Marseille—until someone pulls out their phone to look up cioppino."

I laugh. "That *someone* might be me."

"You've never had cioppino?"

"I don't even know what it is."

"Seafood stew. Tomato broth. A little wine. Slightly spicy. Comes with crusty bread, which is half the reason people order it."

"I don't do spicy."

"Then I suggest the swordfish. Lemon caper butter. Clean, bright, zero heat."

"Sounds good."

The server returns and takes our order. "Something to drink?"

"Viognier?" Michael looks at me for approval. "Pairs well with fish … and writers who don't do spicy."

"Sure." I laugh again, surprised by how easily I do that around him. "You talk about wines like they're human. Like they have moods. Temperaments."

"They do," he says.

"Okay. Explain."

He eases back in his chair. "Take Pinot Noir. It's elegant, but sensitive. Needs just the right climate or it falls apart. Temperamental, but when it's good, it's unforgettable."

I nod. "So... Pinot is the artist."

"Exactly. Cabernet's the CEO. Structured, assertive. Sometimes a little too much. Chardonnay's the overachiever— shows up everywhere, tries to impress, doesn't always know when to stop."

I grin. "And Viognier?"

He picks up one of the glasses the server has delivered. "Doesn't shout. Doesn't try to impress you. It's soft-spoken but layered. Easy to overlook if you're not paying attention."

He rotates the glass slightly in his hand. "But if you slow down, it's all there. Floral, textured, grounded. Knows how to hold its own, just doesn't announce it. It watches everything. Says less. But when it finally speaks, every word matters."

"It's the writer," he says, smiling softly, like he knows exactly what he just said, and meant it.

The calm of feeling understood settles in me. I don't rush to fill the quiet.

"That photo," I say. "The one in your hallway of the woman and the little girl... you looked happy."

The focus in his eyes doesn't waver. "I was."

He takes a sip of his wine, folds his napkin, glancing down at the table like he's considering whether to keep going. "She already had a daughter when we met. The father had left before my daughter was born. Didn't want to be found." He traces the stem of his glass.

The way he says *my daughter* makes me wish I'd been loved like that.

His smile shifts, touched by memory. "I fell in love the moment I saw her sweet little face. She was four in that photo. We were in Aix-en-Provence—her mother's idea. That day, everything felt like it fit. We weren't married, but I loved them like we were."

"That's rare," I say. What I mean is: *you're rare.*

Michael nods, eyes steady on the tablecloth. "Her mother left. Fell for someone else—the shiny kind of love."

"I'm sorry."

"She thought I'd disappear too," he says. "But I didn't. Still showed up for my daughter. Still do. She still calls me Dad."

Tenderness rises in me. I take a sip of water.

"She's twenty-seven now," he smiles. "Works in a bookstore. Still pretends not to like wine."

"Sounds like she got the best part of the deal." I return his smile.

His look softens, and I know he believes me.

Our food arrives, steam rising, everything plated with care.

Michael picks up his fork, glancing at me. "I'm glad you're here."

I meet his eyes. "Me too."

We eat. No rush. No bracing. I let it be good.

8

Too Many Signs

"A sign does not resolve the unknown; it helps you endure it."

-Reid

BY THE TIME I arrive, Mystic is in full interpretive frenzy. Sidewalk chalk arrows point in every direction. Fia greets me with the full-body enthusiasm of a little kid on Christmas morning. She's wearing a layered skirt that looks like it might have belonged to a lampshade in a previous life, paired with a T-shirt that says *Trust the Weird,* and topped by a wide-brimmed hat adorned with tiny dangling moons. She has her *Evidence* notebook in hand.

"You made it!" she says, twirling once for dramatic effect. "Mystic's annual chaos of cosmic clarity."

"That's a lot of Cs," I say.

"Cosmic clarity comes in clusters," she shrugs, "C's are the universe's favorite consonant. Obviously."

She grabs my wrist. "Ready to see the universe flirt with you?"

"Pretty sure the universe ghosted me a long time ago."

She ignores me and gestures broadly to the people milling about, talking to birds, pointing at traffic lights, analyzing shadows. "Today, everything means something."

Someone walks by carrying a handmade sign that reads *Yes, That's the Sign.* A girl in a tutu spins in circles near the fountain and yells, "It's the number three again!" like she just cracked a code.

Fia beams. "Exactly." She turns to me. "Oh—almost forgot." She presses a small card into my hand. Three words in curly gold ink: *No Map Required.*

She winks. "That's your filter for the day. Everyone gets a different one." Then she disappears into the crowd like glitter in a breeze, leaving me surrounded by strangers who seem certain that everything means something.

My *filter for the day*? I have no idea what to do with it. Still, I slip it into my pocket.

Under a tree, a woman scrawls frantically in a notebook. Two people whisper about dryer vent condensation shaped like a heart. I pause longer than I mean to. Not because I see the heart, but because they do.

I wander. I watch.

In front of a bench, a woman stands holding out her sleeve.

"Cupcake," she says, pointing to a splatter of bird poop. "I've been asking for a sign to open a bakery, and look." Her friend doesn't blink. "It's fate."

They hug like something sacred just happened.

"Okay then," I mutter to no one, but apparently out loud.

On the curb, a girl sits cross-legged, journal in her lap, hands stained with blue marker. Eleven, maybe. She looks up. "I'm writing down everything good I see today so I don't forget later."

"I like that." I offer a friendly smile.

She goes back to writing.

Outside a florist shop, a man in his seventies holds up a small daisy in one hand and a photo in the other. "She used to leave daisies on the porch," he tells the florist, his voice steady but worn. "Said it was her way of saying, 'I still like you,' even on the hard days."

He smiles faintly. "Gone twenty-two years, and I'm still looking for her signs."

The tenderness of it stalls me midstep, and I nearly stumble over Fia, crouched on the sidewalk photographing a line of ants.

"A sign?" I ask, stepping around her.

"Obviously," she says, without looking up. "They're carrying a gum wrapper shaped like a heart. That's a triple confirmation."

I look at the crumpled wrapper. If that's a heart, it's one that's been through some things.

"Confirmation of what?" I ask.

Fia stands and dusts off her skirt. "Unclear. But most likely love. Or gum. Could go either way."

She taps her *Evidence* notebook like she's filing it under *Important but Mysterious.* I try to follow her logic and fail completely. Still, I kind of love how certain she is, even when she makes no sense.

We walk a few steps together.

"Seen anything good?" she asks.

"Hmm… a girl writing down everything good she sees. An old man looking for signs from his wife."

Her smile softens. "Yep. That's the real stuff."

"And the ants?"

"Sometimes you just notice what you need to notice." She smiles. "Doesn't have to make sense to anyone else." Then, she tilts her head, listening to something I can't hear. "Hmm." She waves once, like she's dusting me with stardust, and drifts down the block.

Not bothering to ask, I give her a nod in place of goodbye.

It's like watching everyone conduct their own emotional scavenger hunt, and every object is a clue. Ridiculous. And kind of beautiful. Funny, the things people call signs. Part of me gets it—the need to feel like the world is answering back. But, the more signs I see, the less any of them seem to matter. Maybe it's the noise, or the desperation. Either way, all the meaning-making is starting to feel… meaningless.

I pass Deni's spa. A small framed sign sits outside the door. It reads: *"Trust in the Lord with all your heart and lean not on your own understanding."* - Proverbs 3:5

Below it, in what must be Deni's handwriting: *"Look to Jesus for your signs."*

The weight of her belief holds me there. I want to believe in something with that kind of certainty. But right now, it all feels like nonsense. Still, I'd take one sign that feels real.

I keep walking, hoping to feel something that sticks. The crowd thins as I continue away from the mayhem. The sound of declarations and revelations fades behind me. Down a side street, then another, shoes padding against old brick. No signs. No chatter. No cupcake prophecies.

Without meaning to, my pace slows. The street is empty as I round a corner and see a mural stretching across the crumbling side of a building. It feels familiar. Not in the *I've seen it before* way, but like meeting someone and instantly feeling connected; recognition without reason. It's sun-bleached and flaking in places, layers of paint worn by time. Most of it's abstract: shapes, swirls, fragments of color. In the lower left corner, barely visible, a single feather. I step closer. It's faded, brushed in soft white.

Everything in me quiets. Fia's words return:

"They usually show up when you're right where you're supposed to be."

✳

Michael's home, his guest room, doesn't ask anything of me. Not clarity, not conclusions. Just a desk with a view, a soft blanket draped across my lap, and a silence kind enough to let me set the day down and sit with its weight.

Mystic is quiet now. No declarations. Just the faint echo of people trying too hard. With my laptop open, I try to pull something from the day—a thread, a thought, a point.

Nothing.

The girl and her journal. The man with the daisy. The woman and her sleeve full of hope and bird poop. Fia, with her gum-wrapper certainty. Even the feather with its flash of significance. It all swirls together, loud, tender, strange, dramatic… and somehow weightless.

I want it to mean something. I want everything to.

I glance at the compass on the desk. No wrong turns it says. Right now, every turn feels wrong.

I've followed signs before. Held onto them like proof, even when they weren't. The heart-shaped rock I found on the beach the day we got back together. I texted him the photo, convinced life was rooting for us. He didn't text back.

And the song that played—the one we called "our song"—as I was about to leave him again, convinced me to stay. I kept looking for signs, like I didn't already know what I wanted.

Maybe that's the real tragedy—turning life into a scavenger hunt to avoid owning your choices.

Signs. Is any of it real, or are we just meaning-making machines telling stories to feel less alone?

The laptop closed, I lie back on the bed, the image of the feather still faint in my mind, and an unsettling thought: Either I'm on the verge of something or I've wandered completely off the map.

9

The Vineyard

"The life without struggle may be safe, but never remarkable."

-Reid

THE VINEYARD SITS just outside town, hidden behind a line of wind-sculpted trees and a wooden gate. The kind of place you'd never find unless someone told you. Or you're Michael.

Each step grinds the gravel on the path curving past stone markers where fennel pushes through the fence, its sweetness thick in the warm air.

Michael is seated at a weathered table near the vines, a bottle breathing between two glasses.

"Perfect timing," he says, standing to greet me and motioning to the seat across from him.

The view unfurls in front of me; rows of vines stretch wide, light tangled in their leaves, air thick with sun and fruit.

"This place is like an exhale," I say.

Michael smiles. "That's why I come here." He slides a glass across the table. "Some wines tell a story. This one just listens."

The sip is smooth and mellow, like the moment itself. We don't rush into conversation. Bees hum somewhere in the vines as a breeze moves through the rows. No one else around. Just this. Just here.

"Apricot?" I ask, after a second sip.

Michael tilts his head. "Not quite. But I like the ambition."

"What is it?"

"White peach."

I wrinkle my nose. "I was close."

He smirks. "Peach-adjacent. It's in the stone fruit family. I'll give you that."

We chat for a while, then Michael stands and nods toward the vines. "Feel like walking a bit?"

Gravel crunches underfoot as we stroll between the rows. There's something comforting about being around someone who doesn't do small talk.

"Vines produce better grapes in tough soil with less water," he says, brushing a leaf as we walk. "Forces them to dig deeper. The stress brings out depth. Champagne's a perfect example; Veuve Clicquot turned struggle into greatness, becoming what it never could've been in easier soil. Grapes that struggle make the best wine."

My gaze drops to a knot of roots breaking through the soil. Veuve Clicquot, the bottle I once drank with my ex. Struggle sums up my role in that relationship. If Veuve turned hardship into greatness, maybe I can too.

"Guess grapes and people need the same thing," I say.

He smiles as his gaze drifts. "It's true, people do need a little pressure to become their best. But too much strain… it can break you."

"Speaking from experience?" I ask, wondering what he's not saying.

Michael slows, fingertips brushing a leaf as we pass. "There was someone. I thought if I was the calm in her chaos, she'd choose me. But she only wanted what I could give. Not me."

Maybe that's why he offered the guest room so freely. He knows heartbreak. Not the polite nod of sympathy, but the bone-deep recognition of someone who's been there. With him, I don't feel like a guest. I feel like a traveler who staggered in from the same storm. For him, everything's meant to be shared—a bottle, a meal, a home. Maybe even grief.

"You can love someone with everything you've got, and they'll still walk away," I say, hating how much I've given to feel wanted.

"Or worse," he says. "Stay, but never really be in it. I used to think love was something you had to search for. Lately, I think it finds you when you stop looking." A boyish grin sneaks onto his face.

"That look says it all. Who is she?" I nudge his arm, grinning.

"There's someone at the club." He pauses. "She keeps me on my toes, knows more about vintages than half the sommeliers I've trained. We've been talking. Feels easy. So, who knows?"

The air between us clears, my shoulders easing. I never saw him that way, though part of me worried his kindness came with strings. I've known for a while it wasn't like that but hearing it out loud lets me breathe easier.

Seeing him like this makes me smile. "Good. You deserve someone who puts that look on your face."

"So do you," he says.

He stops at a spindly vine, new shoots reaching everywhere. "Young vines overproduce, too much fruit, like they're trying to prove themselves. All that effort makes for a shallow wine no one reaches for."

"I think I've been that vine."

"You can spend a lifetime trying to be easy to love, Anelie," he says. "But that's not the same as being loved."

My chest tightens. He's right. Easy—that's been my whole story. Smile, laugh, don't ask for too much. And what's it ever gotten me? Not love. Just heartache.

Back in the guest room, I sit on the edge of the bed.

Yesterday was noise. People desperate for direction, chaotic … hollow.

Today was calm. Full. No reaching for signs. No reaching for approval.

Most of my life I've tried to be worth choosing, not noticing I left myself behind. I thought if I could just be more agreeable, less complicated, less needy, less *me*, someone would finally choose me. But all I did was slowly disappear inside the relationship, making myself so easy to love, there was nothing left of me to actually love.

Michael's words loop in my head: easy to love, but not loved. I've lived that line—it might as well be tattooed. I don't even know what stopping would look like. Every version of me was a shape I twisted for love. When they left, I blamed the shape.

But today, I didn't twist. I didn't shrink. I stayed me.

The compass waits where I left it, still refusing to give direction. But I didn't need it to.

I lie back on the bed, staring at the ceiling. For once, I'm not analyzing a text, second-guessing my tone, or trying to hold everything together. I'm just here.

No epiphanies. No answers.

But I didn't abandon myself today… and that's something.

10

A Glimpse of the Pattern

"The performance that protects you also erases you."

-Reid

MICHAEL CARRIES THE gift bag, I've got the wine. I chose the gift, and he made it look good. Wrapping was never my thing. Michael makes tissue look elegant.

The tiny house is pure Deni. Market lights loop the porch, and music pulses beneath it all.

Deni swings the door open before we knock. "There you are!" She beams as if we've made her night just by showing up. In a fitted green dress, gold hoops dangling, her heels click like punctuation with every step.

She hugs me tight. "You look amazing. No makeup, and you could still pass for twenty. Rude."

"Meanwhile, I look like a garden gnome in lipstick." She waves a hand at herself.

"Thank you? I think? I've never been complimented and scolded at the same time," I say, half-laughing. "And for the record, you're beautiful. The only gnome thing about you is your size."

She laughs, shaking her head. Her makeup is flawless except for the lip liner: that sharp, unblended ring around her mouth. Why does she do that?

The room is full but not crowded. The table is overflowing with food, and in the corner, a pink cake waits under a glass dome.

"I hope you're hungry," she says.

Michael hands her the gift bag. "From both of us."

She peeks inside and gasps. "Fig and honey body butter? You angel people."

A man shows up with a tray of drinks and locks eyes with Deni. He must be Eric. He's taller than I expected. Good-looking in a way that feels deliberate, he dresses to be looked at. He sets the tray on the counter without acknowledging Michael or me and slides his arm around Deni's waist, the message clear: *mine.*

"You must be Anelie," he says. "I'm Eric."

I nod. "Hi."

He offers a businesslike handshake. "I heard you're the Mystic mystery woman taking over Coffee Compass."

"She's more than that," Deni says, brushing his chest with the back of her hand. "She's a writer. And I know that whatever she writes will be amazing. I mean, look at her, she's got that mysterious, 'I write genius things in coffee shops—vibe."

Eric grins. "Well, I tend to inspire people, so let me know if I need to sign a release form."

Deni gives a forced laugh, glancing down at her glass the way people do when they want to disappear.

We head to the living room, and Michael gets pulled into a conversation with someone about wine pairings and grilled pineapple. I linger at the table, sipping my drink, watching Deni make the rounds like a politician—leaning in when people talk, touching arms, laughing with her whole face. Magnetic. Effortless. But there's a flicker behind it, a shine too practiced. The kind you wear when you're trying to hold it together.

The dining table is piled with serving dishes and finger foods, everyone grazing as they talk. Someone's laughing about a story Deni told earlier about a woman screaming during a massage and blaming it on divine release. I make my way over to Michael, who has slipped free of the pineapple debate and is talking with someone else. He listens with that soft, tilted smile of his, wine glass in hand, like he's in no rush to be anywhere else.

Deni flits between conversations like a finch fueled by espresso, topping off drinks, adjusting trays, and complimenting earrings mid-sentence. Her energy is big and bright.

She brushes past me, sets down a tray, wobbles, then laughs it off. "Don't worry, I'm not drunk—yet. Just been on my feet since five." Then she's gone again, heels clicking toward the stereo.

I spot her a few minutes later, leaning against the door frame next to Eric, her arm laced through his. The music dips and Eric seizes the moment. He raises his glass with the kind of grin that assumes everyone's watching. "To Deni, the only woman I know who can run a business, throw a party, and still lose her phone three times in one night."

Laughter rises. Deni joins in, rolling her eyes as she leans her head on Eric's shoulder.

"She remembers your dog's name and the outfit you wore last year," he continues, "but anything important? Forget it. Still, she's my cute little airhead."

A few laughs sputter across the room, most of them pretending it was funnier than it felt.

"Wow. Charming," I mutter, but not low enough.

Michael glances over my way, the corner of his mouth ticking up.

"Charming's one word for it," he says under his breath, a comment meant only for me.

The brightness flickers out of Deni for a moment, before she pastes it back on, brighter than before, but not fast enough to erase what I saw.

The party is still happening around me, but I'm not in it anymore. I'm watching what lives beneath the busy. The way Deni's eyes dart before they settle. The way she hands out compliments like lifelines, as if being liked is the same as being safe. It's a dance I recognize. The music may be different, but the steps are the same; the dance around a man who needs to be the sun and resents your light for shining.

Michael leans over. "You alright?"

I nod. "Yeah."

But I'm not. I'm remembering every dinner I ever tried to keep light, every time I laughed along with a joke that left a bruise, every room I exited while pretending I hadn't shrunk inside it.

Deni's already moved on to a new conversation, laughing with someone near the dessert table. She's radiant again, touching someone's arm mid-story, refilling a drink like she's being scored on hospitality. But I can still hear the echo of that joke, and the way her laughter caught in her throat.

She keeps it together with practiced positivity. I did it by withdrawing. One performs, the other disappears. Both just trying to stay wanted. I see it now, in her, and in me. And I want none of it. Not the fake smiles. Not the shrinking to fit someone else's life. Not the pretending to be easygoing to feel wanted.

Michael's talking with someone nearby, but I can feel his eyes on me every so often, like he knows I'm not fully here.

Across the room, Deni's laughter is loud and generous. There's nothing in me that wants to criticize her. I get it. I've been there most of my life, pretending everything's fine, telling lies, even to myself, in a desperate attempt to feel loved. And standing here, watching Deni sparkle and strain, I feel done.

The kitchen is quieter, the music muffled by walls and distance. Deni stands at the counter, the cake out from under its dome, slicing carefully. She looks up when I walk in.

"Hey, sugar." Her voice is light. "Did you come looking for me, or to steal a piece of cake before anyone else?"

"Can I do both?"

She laughs softly. "You're my kind of people."

I cross to the counter. "You okay?"

She shrugs without looking up. "I'm fine. Just needed to breathe and cut some cake for you lovely people."

The way she says it makes me think she isn't fine at all.

"I wanted to say something earlier, but it wasn't the right time. That joke Eric made, it wasn't funny."

She lets out a breath, almost a sigh. "He didn't mean anything by it. He was just joking. That's his sense of humor."

"Sure. But sometimes a joke still stings, especially when it's at your expense."

"He jokes like that all the time," she says. "I don't love it, but… it's just how he is."

"I've told myself it was fine, too," I say. "Even when it wasn't. I saw you stumble earlier. You know, pretending you're fine can take a toll on your health."

Her smile drops. Her hand shoots up toward the ceiling, quick and firm. "No. I do not receive that. I rebuke that in the name of Jesus."

"Deni—"

"Nope." She presses the knife into the cake with too much force. "Don't speak that over me. Jesus has my health."

"Sorry," I say. "I wasn't trying to push. My concern just has terrible boundaries."

Her shoulders soften, and a small, breathy laugh escapes. "You know, my cousin says I could sell a punch in the face as a pep talk." Stepping back from the counter, she crinkles her nose. "It's really not a big deal."

I nod, slow. "Okay."

She looks down and brushes at a crumb that isn't there.

"I think you're amazing," I say. "The way you light up every space you walk into, how you make people feel seen. I just wish you were with someone who sees that."

She doesn't answer right away. She rests a hand on the cake server like she's forgotten what it was for. "Don't worry about me," she says, softer.

"Okay, I just didn't want to leave without saying something. That's all."

The silence stretches before she bumps her shoulder into mine. "You're sweet. Now, you want cake or not?"

I smile. "Absolutely."

11

The Temptation Deepens

"The burden is not confusion, but the weight of
unwelcomed truth."

-Reid

STANDING IN MICHAEL'S kitchen, still in my pajamas, I'm calm, grounded, with no laptop, no urging myself to be productive, sipping my second cup of coffee. My phone buzzes. No words. Just a video. From him.

I tap it open. The ten second video is a wide shot of the ocean from the balcony of a beachside hotel. The wind stirs the camera mic and the horizon shimmers like it did that morning we had mimosas at sunrise, swearing we'd never go back to real life. I watch it over and over again.

I tell myself it's just a video. Maybe he meant it for someone else or hit send by accident. And then I do something I don't understand even as I'm doing it. I tap the heart. No words. No commitment. But not silence.

My stomach tightens. I miss what it felt like to be wanted, even if it was all conditional. I flip the phone over, face down.

Reaching for my laptop, I open the document *Signs* and scroll back through what I've written—all the lines about stillness and disappearing. Some of it feels true. Some of it feels like I'm still growing into it.

The phone rings. Seeing his name tugs at the part of me that still wants it to mean love. On the third ring, I cave.

"Hey, didn't think you'd pick up," my ex says, voice yielding, like I've stepped into a part of him he doesn't usually show. The silence stretches as he waits for me to speak. I don't.

"Do you remember that trip? We had so much fun. I miss you so much." He pauses, then says, "That video popped up on my phone today. You know how it does that? *'On this day…'* or whatever. I don't know how to turn it off, but it won't stop showing me memories of you."

He laughs like it's out of his hands, as if it means something. "That trip, I keep thinking about it. I got you that necklace with the turtle pendant. I remember thinking, *God, I could do forever with this woman.*" He pauses, waiting for me to fill the space. I almost do.

"I know I messed up," he continues. "I took you for granted. I wanted to call sooner, but I figured you had moved on. And then that video showed up and I—I had to call."

I ache to believe him. But I know the pattern. Whatever he feels now won't last. He always goes back to who he is, and I'm left holding nothing.

Before I can respond, he rushes ahead. "Please tell me there's still a chance for us. No, don't answer. Just think about it, okay? Can you at least tell me you'll think about it?"

I would've heard it differently a few weeks ago. Back when I was still waiting for him to explain it all in a way that made sense. Now, I just hear the cycle starting over. He means every word, right up until he doesn't.

"I'll understand if you say no, but, I just… " he says. "I've been thinking about you. About us. A lot. And I guess I wanted to know if, if maybe you'd be open to seeing me."

He waits. "No pressure," he adds, softening the edges. "I just want to see you. Just to talk."

I don't know why, but I say yes. Not because I want him or even believe him. It's not even hope. It's what I learned early—avoid conflict, let other people decide when it's over. Be agreeable. Kind. Part of me doesn't want to let him down. Part of me wants to feel wanted. And part of me—maybe the biggest part—feels done. Not with him, exactly. Just done waiting for him to say the right words to make forgiving him feel justified when I know better.

He says he'll text me. A time. A place. Like it's casual. Like I don't know what he's trying to make happen.

"I love you, Anelie," he says before hanging up. "Even if you don't believe it."

"I believe you," I say. And I do—believe he means it. I just don't want the version of love he's offering. I set the phone down, regret already curling through me for saying yes.

The kitchen is silent, like the moment is waiting to see what I'll do next. This is the part where I used to unravel. Where I'd replay the call a dozen times, dissect every word, search for meaning in his tone, his timing, the length of the pause before *I love you*. This is where I used to collapse.

Not this time.

I carry my mug to the sink, rinse it out, dry my hands on the dish towel that smells faintly of citrus. A bird lands on the railing outside the window, then flits away. No "sign." Just a bird.

I exhale.

The *Signs* document is still open. I begin typing. *It's not clarity she needs. She needs to stop begging for clarity by asking questions she already knows the answers to. She's not confused. She needs to stop chasing what hurts.*

12

The Compass Is Broken

"When direction is absent, forward remains."

-Reid

MICHAEL'S ALREADY GONE this morning. Last night he mentioned a date after work tonight, leftovers in the fridge. "Don't wait up," he'd said, a smile tugging at the corner of his mouth.

There's a note next to the coffee maker: *You don't need to write to be a writer. You only need to notice. - Michael*

I don't feel like noticing anything.

The *Signs* document is open. I've read the last paragraph five times. I can't tell if I like it anymore, if it's honest, or if I just want it to be true. Yesterday it felt brave. Today it feels forced, like a version of me I wanted to become.

Fingers on the keyboard, I wait for a spark of clarity. Nothing.

My coffee goes lukewarm. The silence is starting to feel like a verdict. I scroll through what I've written: half paragraphs, trailing thoughts, unfinished ideas. A sentence that once felt profound now reads as trying too hard.

Instead of writing, I retrace the choices I've made and the patterns I let repeat.

The married counselor who patted his lap and said, *"Sit here."* I felt the red flag and sat anyway. Two years of swallowing discomfort followed.

The cheating alcoholic who called it "transparency" when he flaunted explicit texts from other women our first week together. Three years later, he took another woman on the trip I planned.

The signs were always there.

I've called it love. But it was always something else. Something that required me to disappear just enough to tolerate it.

I sit back, hands folded in my lap. I don't even feel angry. I just feel tired.

I move from the table to the couch without thinking. The sun has shifted, casting a long slice of light across the floor. I don't bother to close the curtains.

I scroll through my phone. Close it, open it, check my email. Nothing. Keep scrolling.

His texts are still there. I never deleted them.

The one where he said, *"I've never met anyone like you."* The one where I said, *"Be honest with me,"* and he replied, *"I always am."*

My stomach twists, not with sadness, but with disappointment in the version of me who read those words like scripture, looking for proof of devotion.

I set the phone face down, like that does anything. I should cancel, send a text: *"Actually, I don't think meeting is a good idea."* I type it. Delete it. Canceling feels like a decision, and I'm not ready for that either.

Back at the laptop, the screen glares at me, blank and judgmental. This isn't a block. This is something else.

An undoing.

My fingers scroll to the section where I once wrote, *"Sometimes the real sign is the one you don't want to see."* I don't know if I agree with myself anymore. I close the laptop. I've been here before. This exact feeling. It's the part of the pattern where I doubt myself; maybe I imagined the pain, maybe I overreacted. Maybe I wasn't brave yesterday, just riding a moment of confidence I can't sustain.

I pull a blanket over my lap and sink into the couch. Outside, a branch taps the window, slow and irregular, like it wants me to notice. I don't move.

※

Night settles in and I'm still on the couch. The room is dark, quiet, except for the hum of the house and the dull ache of circling thoughts. I should eat, or move, or get up. I don't.

Why did I say yes? Maybe I should text him and cancel. Or go—prove something to myself. Not sure what.

Eventually, I push the blanket off to break the heaviness and head to the guest room.

The compass looks less symbolic now, just an object on a desk. I hold it in both hands and close my eyes.

"What am I supposed to do? Where am I supposed to go?" I ask out loud.

No answer. No whispered magic. Just silence. The kind that feels like being abandoned.

I set it down and step away, hating how badly I wanted it to answer.

On the edge of the bed, I stare into the dark.

13

A Hint of Clarity

*"Your existence is the invitation; nothing more is
required."*

-Reid

MY USUAL TABLE—the one with the daisy—waits for me. I
touch the compass in my pocket and consider leaving it on the
counter.

Today I didn't come for the coffee. I brought my laptop.
I'm not sure I'll write. I don't have a plan, I just wanted to be
here, surrounded by the buzz of other people's lives. Close
enough to not feel alone, and maybe, if stirred, the space to write
in what I now consider my "office."

The little white flower, slightly wilted, but still upright.
A metaphor for me in this moment, a bit withered but still
standing. I almost wonder if Mystic left it here on purpose, to

see if I'm paying attention. I roll my eyes at myself. But I'm not completely ruling it out.

On the board behind the counter, Reid's message awaits:

If you stopped asking where to go,
would you finally hear where you are? -Reid

My gaze lingers. It's strange how often those words match what's going on inside me.

Resa appears with two mugs. She sets one in front of me—coffee with cream, just the way I like it—and slides into the seat across from me like the conversation's already been decided.

I nod at the cup. "Thanks."

She lifts her mug and looks out the window, letting the moment stretch as if she already knows what's coming.

I want to pretend everything's fine, but I know better. The compass rests in my palm. "I should give this back."

She glances at it, then back at me.

"It was never mine."

I almost ask what she means but let it go. "I thought it might somehow point me in the right direction."

She closes my fingers over it. "Maybe it's here to remind you that you already know the way. Some things are only meant to pass through us."

Unsure if she means the compass, or something else, I leave it in the middle of the table.

She leans back, eyes steady on her mug. "I still talk to him sometimes when no one's around. I don't expect an answer, but it makes the room feel less empty."

The son she lost. The memory hushes me. Maybe that's what she meant about the compass—some things just keep you company in the emptiness. But I'm not sure comfort without answers is enough for me.

Out the window, the crosswalk signal blinks, though no one's waiting to cross.

"I don't even know if I believe in signs anymore," I say. "Or anything."

Resa gives a faint smile. "Do you know what your name means?"

"Anelie? No."

"It means 'God's favorite.'"

A hollow laugh slips out. "Seriously?"

"You don't have to accept it," says Resa. "Just let the possibility stay there for a minute."

It sounds absurd. But then I remember something I haven't thought of in years. I shake my head, half-smiling. "I had a friend who, every time something good happened, we'd joke we were God's favorite. *Front-row parking again? Clearly, I'm God's favorite.*"

Resa smiles softly.

"I didn't actually believe it," I say. "It was just a thing we said. A joke."

"And now?" she asks.

"The fact my name means that? I don't know. I've never felt like anyone's favorite."

"What if we're all God's favorite? What if everyone's chosen. No exceptions."

"Chosen for what?"

"To be here. To be loved."

I study her face, trying to decide how I feel about what she's saying.

The compass sits there, silent in a way that feels different.

"What if being 'God's favorite' is just another way of saying you belong?" she says. "And what if your name is simply meant to remind you that love wants you here. As you are."

Love wants me here. The words settle under my ribs. "You believe that?"

"I believe real love isn't something you work for. It's what you are."

Love is something... I am. The idea feels true.

Resa continues, "God's favorite doesn't mean you're more loved than others. But that you're never unloved."

Never unloved. I try to let that in.

"I was named after Saint Teresa of Ávila," she says, "who believed spiritual life wasn't about rules, but about love. And over time, I've grown into my name."

"And Anelie... *Love wants me here,*" I say. I'd like to grow into mine.

Resa stands slowly, mug in hand, giving me a soft smile as she heads toward the counter.

I remain seated long after she's gone. I'm not sure I have anything figured out, but I'm listening. I slide the compass back into my pocket.

Not as a sign. As a reminder.

That night, I sleep hard.

In a dream, I'm in a room I've never seen but somehow know. Honey-colored walls, windows open to the wind. No furniture. Warm wood floors under my feet. Alone, but not. Something holds me. Not arms. Just presence.

You belong.

Two words. They hold everything: love, worth, presence. It doesn't come as a thought. It settles in as if it's always been there: *You belong, because you exist. You are loved as you are. Nothing to do. Just receive. You're not alone. You never were.*

Warmth spreads through my chest, like an exhale after too long holding my breath. The compass is in my hand. I don't need it to tell me where to go. I know where I am.

I wake before dawn. I remember, being four years old, too young to question, back when something bigger just *was*. Not an answer to find, but a presence I trusted.

14

The Winery

"The end of the lie is the refusal to uphold it."

-Reid

THE WINERY IS a short drive from town. The invite was simple—ladies only. Deni had texted: *This Saturday, fabulous ladies + wine and sunshine = wellness. Obviously. Be there.* A couple days later, she followed up: *Heads-up, Eric's tagging along. Long story.* No explanation. No smiley face.

The tasting room is airy and rustic—brick walls, wood counters, and a high ceiling overhead. Laughter drifts in from the patio, glasses clinking, music humming low—strings, soft vocals. Outside, a long table waits, already half full of people I don't know.

A woman with a clipboard greets me. "Here for the tasting?"

I nod. "I'm with Deni."

"Of course," she says, smiling. "She's running a little behind." Her tone implies *this is not unusual.*

She shows me to a seat halfway down the table. A wine glass waits beside a folded tasting menu with words like *floral nose* and *hints of stone fruit.*

The host pours the first wine, a Sauvignon Blanc. She talks through its notes. Distracted, I catch only fragments, as I look around for Deni and Eric.

When Deni first texted to say Eric was coming, I almost bailed. I've already seen enough of him to know I don't enjoy his company. I came for Deni.

Across the table, a woman jokes that it tastes like fruit and river rocks. I laugh politely. Swirl. Sip. Try to look like I belong.

The second wine is poured before Deni arrives. Still no Eric.

Someone murmurs something about a "mineral finish." Another keeps inhaling her glass until it's awkward. I nod along, but my focus is fixed on the door.

A few more guests drift in. The host explains the next pour—red, earthy, grapes I've never heard of. I take a small sip, let it rest on my tongue. Soil and sun.

Behind me, a woman asks, "Is he still with that girl from the spa?" Her voice is hushed, but not enough. Another woman answers, *"Deni? Yeah. For now."* Then they laugh.

I'm not surprised, but disappointed all the same.

The host announces a short break, ten minutes before the final flight. I excuse myself and head toward the tasting room. I escape the polite strangers and secondhand gossip in a small, sunlit restroom. It's all too much—makes me wonder if I belong here at all.

At the sink, I breathe, then again, before pushing open the door.

On the way back from the restroom, Eric's laugh finds me. I slow before the patio door. His voice is low and smooth, designed to charm, threading between bursts of conversation.

At the edge of the main room, he stands near a small table. A blonde woman—early twenties, glossy lips, a black dress cut to invite eyes—leans in smiling, laughing too hard, too long.

His chin tucked, eyes narrowed, like her every word is rare and brilliant. Pure player move. Their phones are out. A few taps. A screen tilted to confirm. Her fingertips brush his chest and he leans in just enough to say yes without saying anything. Not one betrayal, just a thousand little permissions he gives himself. The lines crossed are far enough to sting, but not enough to name. Not proof. Just cracks in the story you keep trying to believe.

I stand there a moment longer, my breath shallow. Through the glass, I see Deni on the patio, laughing with a group at the end of the table, face tipped to the sun, hand curled around her glass. She looks happy, at ease. Beautiful in a way she won't claim. Watching her laugh, I ache. I know how fast joy unravels when you're clinging to what you wish was true. I've been there. I want to warn her, protect her somehow. But it never ends with thanks. It ends with them choosing the lie.

And right now, the past is too loud—the charm, the deflection, the ache of knowing and not wanting to. Before, I would've stayed. Leaving felt scarier than pretending. But now, staying feels impossible. There's no room left in me to keep protecting illusions. She has no idea what's happening in the next room. And I won't be the one to dim that light. I'm walking away before I'm asked to pretend.

I step back and head for the exit.

Outside, each step forward feels lighter. I slide into my car and rest my hands on the wheel, not ready to turn the key.

The memory finds me. A bar.

My ex leaning toward a woman I didn't know. His voice low. Her laugh too warm. Me, pretending not to notice. The knot in my stomach tightening anyway. The text I found the next day. His claim it was business. The way I believed him—because I wanted to.

This time, I don't stay to keep the peace. This time, I choose myself.

No confrontation. No explanation. Just the decision to stop abandoning me.

The car rolls forward over gravel as I pull out of the lot, each crackle under the tires a door closing behind me. The window slides halfway down and the wind brushes my face. The sun has dipped behind the trees. I leave the music off. Quiet is what I want.

Half a mile out, my phone buzzes in the passenger seat. At a stop sign, I glance at the screen.

Hey, this is Jen. We looked for you. Deni gave me your number. She collapsed and is at the hospital. Not sure what happened. She wanted you to know.

My stomach drops. I text back quickly. *Thank you. Please keep me posted.*

Another mile passes, the silence pressing, not soothing. Both hands on the wheel, trying to steady the storm inside me. It could be anything. Dehydration. A panic attack. Something worse. But deep down I know—it's the weight of carrying too much for too long.

I pull into Michael's driveway and check my phone. A message from Deni:

I'm fine. Just tired, that's all. Don't worry.

I stare at the screen. It's exactly what I would've said once. I know this collapse. I've lived it. It's the cost of avoiding a truth you can't face.

This is what happens when you only feel steady if they are. When the person beside you only wants the version of you that makes them feel better. When you swallow the truth to keep things working. And when your body pays for your silence.

Sometimes the collapse isn't about one moment. It's about every moment you didn't let yourself leave.

I know better now. And that changes everything.

15

The Quiet Return

"You are never without direction; only without trust."

-Reid

MICHAEL OPENS THE door before I reach it. "Welcome back."

"Glad to be back." Air moves easier through my lungs.

He studies me, then steps aside. Inside, the house wraps around me—gentle, asking nothing.

He glances toward the kitchen. "You want a glass of something?"

"Yeah."

A bottle waits on the counter, already breathing beside two glasses, like it was never a question. He pours and hands me one without ceremony.

"Complex at first," he says with a wink. "But finishes strong."

I give a faint smile. "Like me, I hope."

We move to the living room, taking our usual spots. Dusk brushes the walls in a soft salmon glow. I cradle the glass in both hands. "I left early."

Michael nods, no surprise in his eyes. "You okay?"

"I am now. I just… I saw something. And I couldn't pretend it didn't matter."

He waits, not pressing.

I rest my glass on the arm of the sofa. "It's strange how easy it is to lie to ourselves. A little at a time, playing along, swallowing the feeling, brushing it off." I pause. "Until that's just how you live."

Michael nods. "Little things become a life."

"They do. And not just emotionally—physically. Self-betrayal shows up in your stomach, your sleep, your energy."

He nods. "Ignore it long enough, and it finds another way out."

I look down at the wine in my glass. "I used to think I was strong for putting up with everything, holding it in, smoothing it over, doing whatever it took to keep the peace. But if it costs you your health, what kind of strength is that?"

Michael leans in. "People who choose what brings them peace, instead of just keeping the peace, end up happier, healthier. The ones who sacrifice their own peace to keep everyone else's—"

"Collapse," I finish.

He nods again. "Eventually."

I think of Deni. The way her body gave up. The way she texted *Just tired,* like she'd swallowed the words she needed to say.

"I'm not doing that anymore," I say quietly. "I won't disappear just to make someone else comfortable."

Michael's lips curve, soft and knowing. He sets his glass down, giving the moment space.

"I'm impressed," he says, nodding with the pride of a vintner watching a vine take root. "That takes courage. Courage chooses to move beyond fear."

The words startle me. My mother used to say that. Usually when I least expected it, after I told the truth about something hard to admit, or stood my ground when it would've been easier to cave. She'd cheer me on to do the scary thing: *Courage chooses to move.*

I'd forgotten how much it meant. How much I needed to hear it now. Maybe it's a sign. A nod. Life saying, *Yes, keep going.* Not loud or dramatic. Just clear.

I step outside into the cool evening air and walk. My body leads, my thoughts trailing behind.

The town is easy, the way small towns are at the end of the day—doors half-closed, porch lights flicking on, the clatter of dishes behind screen doors.

I pass the bakery, its window dark, a faint trace of cinnamon still in the air. The bookstore, its hand-painted rose compass above the door, offers a kind of reassurance: *Yes. Carry on.* Fingers close around the compass in my pocket. What is it I keep hoping for? Direction, reassurance?

I cross the street. Coffee Compass is closed for the night. Through the window, I see Reid's words on the board:

Do signs guide us?
Or do they remind us that we already know? -Reid

An echo of what I've already begun to understand. His message, as always, is right on cue.

A couple walks past with a dog. The woman nods. The dog wags, as if it knows something.

I keep walking.

At the end of the street, the harbor opens up. Boats bob gently in the fading light. The breeze carries a softness to it as it dances around me—a nudge to take the next step.

At the end of the dock, a weathered bench waits. I pull out my phone.

His name is there. Still waiting to pull me back into something I've already outgrown.

I tap the thread and scroll. Not to remember what he said, but how it made me feel. The hope. The excuses. The way I tried to call confusion love.

There's one old message where I apologized for needing anything. I remember typing it and hating myself for it. And the messages where I laughed at things that didn't feel funny. And the most recent ones. One says he misses me. The next—no pressure, just wants to talk.

I press and hold the message thread. Tap delete. Block the number. The screen goes dark. He's gone.

I'm not going back. And he's not coming with me. I don't feel sorry. I don't feel scared. I feel... here.

The breeze picks up slightly. A flag across the harbor flutters once. I take the compass from my pocket as Resa's words rise again: *"Maybe it's here to remind you, you already know the way."*

Maybe I do know the way. Maybe I always have. I just had to stop begging for answers long enough to hear them.

I glance in the direction of Michael's house. The man who offered me a room without asking for anything in return. Who cared for me with fresh flowers in the guest room, coffee waiting each morning, dinners paired with wine and gentle wisdom—breadcrumbs leading me back to myself.

He saw me unraveling and didn't try to fix it, just stayed near while I figured out how to be whole on my own.

I didn't plan any of it. I wasn't searching for it or chasing it. I haven't done anything to earn it or to make it stay. It just showed up. I showed up. Maybe that's what love looks like when it's real. Just there—stable, gentle, unmistakable once you've stopped mistaking everything else for it.

I open the *Signs* document on my phone and add one more line: *The moment I stopped seeking love, love found me.*

My phone buzzes.

Deni: *Hey girl. How's the writing going?*

Me: *Great, actually.* 😊

Deni: *I'd love to read it! Meet me at the spa tomorrow. I'll close up early. 3pm? I'll bring the wine.*

I smile at the screen. I haven't seen her since the winery, since her collapse. Maybe tomorrow will give me a chance to find out what happened.

Me: *You sure?*

Deni: *Positive. Can't wait!*

Something warm spreads through me. Friendship. She's eager to read it. That means everything. Sharing my writing is exciting and scary. But with Deni, it feels safe.

The water ahead ripples without hurry, reflecting the sky. A gull lifts off in the distance. A buoy knocks in rhythm with the tide. Beneath the bench, something pale near my foot. I lean forward.

A feather. Slightly curled, worn at the edges, resting against my shoe.

Fia's voice echoes: *"If you see a feather, you're exactly where you're supposed to be."*

I smile. My fingers find the compass in my pocket. A gentle *Yes.* And then, like a whisper rising from within me—*The direction is inside you.*

I smile again, stay a moment longer, then turn—this time toward *home.*

16

The Completion

"To choose yourself is to bring the seeking to rest."

-Reid

THE HOUSE IS still, the scent of coffee waiting to brew drifting toward me as I pad into the kitchen. The kindness of something so simple continues to move me.

My laptop under my arm, mug in hand, I step onto the patio, the screen door clicking shut behind me. I open the document, *Signs,* scroll to the beginning and skim. A few lines tug, but I don't edit. I just let them be what they are: honest. This wasn't a book I planned to write. Part memoir, part essay. It started as a way to understand, a way to tell the truth without justifying it.

It hits me: I wasn't following signs. I was grasping for validation, for any excuse to disappear, to make myself easy enough to be wanted. Now, no man is calling me. No apology is pulling me back. No voice is louder than my own. For the first time, I'm not waiting. Not for love. Not for clarity. Not for a sign.

I type: *The sign that mattered most was the one she ignored: The ache every time she left herself behind.*

I stare at the sentence. A final puzzle piece snaps into place. I type:

She discovers that the only real "sign" worth following is the one that leads her back to herself.

That love isn't earned through self-sacrifice, but what flows when she's rooted in truth.

That "looking for signs" was a longing to trust her own voice.

That intuition isn't in the stars or symbols, it's in the moments she stops trying to convince herself.

That home isn't a place, a person, or a purpose, it's knowing she doesn't need to go missing in someone else's story to be loved.

Save. Print. It's done.

Inside, the printer hums to life. The rhythm of slow stacking pages reaches from Michael's office.

I lay the manuscript on the patio table, placing the compass beside it. Two objects. One journey.

A compass with no needle. A book called *Signs*. Both pointing to the same place.

My phone buzzes.

Deni: *Hey, lady. I hate to do this, but I have to cancel. Eric's upset about something and needs me. Rain check?*

I stare at the neat stack of paper, notes I scribbled just for her.

I type back: *No problem. Another time.*

I'm not even mad. Just… aware. I used to do this too—drop everything for a man. I told her it was fine, but it's not. Because I know that woman. I was her for decades.

I slide the book into my bag, like tucking in a child who deserves better company.

Resa appears from behind the counter. My little corner sanctuary is waiting for me.

"Morning," she says, with that knowing smile of hers.

I nod. "Morning."

"You wrote something." It's not a question.

I smile as I pull the stack of pages from my bag. "I did."

She sets a scone on a plate and slides it across the counter. "May I see it?"

I hesitate for a second, then hand it over. "Sure."

She holds it gently, like it's alive. Reads the title page. Then flips to a spot a few pages in and lingers there. After a moment, she reads one line aloud: "*She thought she needed someone to choose her. But when she finally chose herself, she already had everything she was looking for."*

She closes the stack. "That line alone is why others need to read this."

"I wrote it for me. I'm not sure it's anything more than that."

"Exactly why it's worth sharing," she says. "It's vulnerable. It simply tells the truth."

Fia pops her head around the corner from the back hallway, holding a carton of oat milk like it's a magic wand. "Ooh!" she says, eyes lighting up at the stack of pages. "Is that the book?"

I laugh. "The book?"

She nods, serious. "Yep. Saw it in my toast this morning. Little burn mark shaped like a hardcover." She steps closer, squinting at the pages. "That's it. Knew I'd run into it today."

Resa glances up, a soft smile playing at the edge of her mouth. "The universe does have its ways."

Fia grins. "Told you." Then adds, "Hope it mentions birds. Or compasses."

Resa folds her arms, then softens. "I know someone," she says, turning serious again. "An independent publisher. Local. Does small-run, mission-driven stuff. Memoir. Essays. They're always looking for work with soul."

My heart flutters, a deep, certain yes from somewhere inside.

"You don't have to answer right now," she says. "But if you're open to it, I'd love to pass it along."

I glance down at the manuscript and nod slowly. "I didn't realize I wanted that, but… I think I do."

Resa's smile deepens. "Then we'll see what happens."

Fia hums and waves her fingers like she's casting a spell. "You heard her. It's begun."

I laugh again, but my gaze drifts back to the pages. A memory tugs. I was ten.

Sitting cross-legged on the floor of our tiny apartment, scribbling thoughts into a notebook, beside my leaning tower of library books. One of my mom's friends had stopped by, the one I liked the most. She asked what I wanted to be when I grew up.

"A writer," I'd said without hesitation. I loved writing. Not stories. Just… what I saw. What I felt. It was how I listened to myself.

My mom's friend touched my hand and said, "I can see it." A book cover flashed in my mind, my name across it. And I knew—someday, somehow, my words would matter.

I hold out the stack to Resa—an offering. I didn't write it to be published. But now, maybe, letting it live beyond me is part of completing it.

Outside Coffee Compass, I see Deni across the street in front of the spa, phone in hand, sunglasses pushed to the top of her head. As always, she's put-together, but there's a stiffness to her stance.

She sees me and brightens, but her smile doesn't quite reach her eyes. "Hey! There she is. Lookin' all peaceful and glowy. What are you drinking, can I have a gallon of it?"

I cross the street. "Just caffeine and fresh air."

"Unfair," she says, and gives me a quick hug. "I'm over here running on stress and fumes."

I step back, meeting her eyes. "Are you okay?" This is the first real chance I've had to ask since she collapsed.

She waves a dismissive hand. "Please." She rolls her eyes with a dramatic sigh. "I told you, I'm just tired. Or hormones. Whatever. I'm fine."

I hold her gaze. "Deni."

Her eyes dart sideways. "Don't 'Deni' me. I already gave myself a talking-to in the mirror. Gonna drink more water, sleep at night, maybe stop skipping meals like a fool." She says it lightly, but her expression falters for a second.

"How are you *really*?" I ask.

She shrugs. "Tired. But, you know, who isn't?" After a pause, she adds, softer. "Some men just know how to suck the joy out of an afternoon of wine and cheese."

"Something happen at the winery?" I say, already suspecting Eric was the cause of her body waving the white flag.

She hesitates, then shrugs. "Well, everything was fine till Mister Business Cards got all flirty with Miss Spray-Tan-Peek-a-Boob Dress."

Without meaning to, I fall quiet, doing what Michael does—no advice, no rescue. Just here. Steady. Trusting she'll find her own way through.

"I might be overthinking it, but some woman walks up to our table, reaches out all slow, drags her fingers down his arm like she's petting a cat, and says—" she lowers her voice to a breathy imitation—"'Be sure to call me.'"

She straightens. "Call you for what, ma'am?" Shrugs. "He says it was business. I say, if it's business, why's she purring?" She exhales. "Whole night went sideways after that. We got into a huge fight."

I remember the sick twist in my stomach watching my ex charm someone else in front of me and call it harmless. Swallowing it down, not wanting to seem insecure. Convincing myself it wasn't a big deal. But now? It's like watching a rerun of a show that once wrecked me. The ache's not there anymore. I see it for what it is: A woman seeking love from someone who never offered it.

Deni lights up rooms for everyone else, but dims herself for Eric.

My voice softens. "I'm sorry, Deni." I mean it. I am sorry for her. But her cancelling on me still stings. She's the first friend I've trusted with something real in years. I can't blame her. I've done the same thing. Ditched friends, chosen the man who didn't deserve it. I get it.

Deni's eyes glisten with everything she's not saying. "I'm fine. I'm just making a big deal out of nothing."

I know she's not fine, but if she says it out loud, something has to change, and I'm sure change doesn't feel like an option.

"If it hurts, it matters," I say. Then Michael's words come to mind, and I continue, "Ignore it long enough, and it finds another way out... like maybe collapsing at a winery?"

She nods slowly, eyes glassy, then gives her head a brief shake to scatter the moment before it settles too deep. She snaps her fingers and points to the sky, placing her order with God. "Well, if stress takes me out, I better be buried cute—with pumps and lip liner."

She straightens, restless on her feet. "Anyway, Saturday at seven. Girls' night at the spa. A monthly thing. Wine, tea, bougie snacks, and chocolate that fixes nothing but makes everything feel better."

I raise a brow.

She leans in. "We sit around, talk, vent, laugh too loud, and drink too much wine." Then, softer. "It's the only time some of these ladies get to relax. Be around other women who get it."

I give a smile that says, *That's beautiful of you.*

"So," she says, tipping her head. "You in? We already like you and you've got cute shoes. That's pretty much the criteria."

I smile. "Sure."

"Good," she says. Then, almost shy, "You're easy to be around. Got that calm thing—makes me feel less nuts. Like chamomile tea. But, you know... a person."

I open my mouth to respond, but she's already opening the spa door. "Okay, gotta run. See you Saturday. You're my emotional support writer now. You gotta be there."

She disappears inside before I can say anything else.

I laugh. *Emotional support writer, huh.* I don't hate the idea. Maybe that's exactly what I am.

On my way to the harbor, glimpses of life flicker through windows—someone setting a table, someone tending a plant, someone laughing into a phone. I cross the footbridge and take the long way around the docks, letting the rhythm of my steps match the water's unhurried sway.

Signs started as fragments. No shape in mind, only the pull to write something I needed to understand. A love letter to myself. And now it's a book. And maybe Resa's right, it's meant to be shared.

At the far end of the dock, I lean against the railing, held by Mystic—no longer just a place, but a companion.

What if someone sees themselves in my book and feels less alone? Maybe that's the whole point.

The wind lifts a wisp of hair from my face. I close my eyes. It seems life has been conspiring for me all along. Toward this town, these people, this moment. It's just me, and I've never felt less alone. Maybe that's all the book is meant to do—help others to feel less alone.

Deni called me an *emotional support writer*. I think she might be right.

I open the Notes app on my phone and type: *The book isn't about finding love. It's about choosing myself, instead of rejecting who I am to feel wanted.*

17

A Gathering of Women

"The gift of gathering is not answers, it's belonging."

-Reid

"OKAY, LADIES, BOUGIE snacks, and of course, wine. Help yourselves and get comfy." Deni waves toward the spread: a tray of cheese, grapes, crackers, and a bowl of Godiva dark chocolates. Wine bottles stand ready, along with a carafe of cucumber water and an ornate teapot next to mugs.

The spa is transformed: soft glow of candles fills the room, plush chairs, and a small sectional arranged in a cozy circle. An inviting haven for tonight's gathering.

Fia giggles and chooses a mug. "Tea feels mystical tonight. If I start floating, just go with it."

"I'll take mystical… without the floating," Resa says, pouring tea into her mug.

Laughter ripples softly around the group, relaxing the mood. Everyone settles into their seats with snacks. Deni is bouncing energetically between each woman, a force of restless kindness. But beneath it, something is off.

One of the women looks at Deni and says, "Where do you get all that energy?"

Deni smirks. "According to Eric, I'm best in small doses, preferably silent ones."

Before I can stop myself, the words slip out—"Why do you let someone who doesn't even see you decide how you see yourself?"

She freezes for half a second, then waves it off with a little snort. "Please. He sees plenty. He just wishes I came with a mute button."

But the pause was there. A crack in the mask. I don't push it.

"Alright," Deni says, finally dropping into a chair, wine in hand. She briefly introduces everyone—Resa, Fia, the mom named Melanie who stopped by the spa the day I met Deni, and a woman whose name I've already forgotten but recognize from the Follow the Signs event.

"First, I want to thank you, Deni," says Melanie. "For providing this lovely space for us to come together and support each other. As a stressed-out single mom, these gatherings have been a lifeline for me."

We all nod, a few smiles offered in support.

"I, um, I started therapy," Melanie continues quietly. "I never thought I'd be that woman, you know? The one who needs help. But turns out, that's everyone. It's been hard, but good."

"Strength isn't never needing help," Resa says, "True strength is allowing it."

Melanie exhales. Then, a grin spreads across her face. "Speaking of help, I finally got into that art class I've been applying for." She shakes her head, still smiling. "I was talking to Resa about it one morning, saying how I didn't know if my application was strong enough. Next thing I know, Reid offers to take a look at it. He handed it back the next day, full of suggestions, stuff I hadn't even thought to include. I made the edits, sent it in, and... I'm in."

"That's great news," says, Resa.

A ripple of congratulations moves around the room.

"I never could've gotten in without Reid's help," says Melanie.

"Yep, that's Reid, our stealthy hero," Fia chimes in.

"A kindness ninja." Deni chuckles and nudges Fia.

The laughter lingers, then thins into something softer. Everyone settles a little deeper.

"How are things with your sister?" says Melanie, eyes fixed on Resa.

"We haven't talked in a while," says Resa. "She wants me to stop mentioning Tony. For her, moving on means trying to forget. For me, it means carrying him with me. I know it's hard for her. She was caring for him that day. But I can't erase my boy to make her comfortable. So we don't talk much."

The group goes still. Even Fia stops fidgeting. Deni shifts, like she might speak but doesn't. Bird Poop Lady from the signs event reaches over and gives Resa's arm a small squeeze.

"I didn't know his name was Tony," I say. "My brother's name was Tony. It means 'priceless one.'"

Resa's eyes soften, finding mine. "Seems we both know the value of that name."

The room settles for a breath, then Bird Poop Lady leans forward, eyes brightening as she sets down her wine glass. "Okay, so I have news. Remember Mystic's 'Signs' event a few weeks ago?" She glances around as several heads nod in recognition. "So, we're all strolling along, everyone is finding feathers, special numbers, inspiring graffiti—all the good stuff. Not me. I'm wandering along, feeling left out, thinking, 'Wow, even signs skip me.' Then out of nowhere, splat." She laughs, shaking her head. "Yep. Bird poop, right on my sleeve. But wait—it wasn't just any bird poop. It landed perfectly shaped like a cupcake. Like, absolutely unmistakably cupcake-shaped."

Fia's eyes widen dramatically. "Cosmic intervention by pigeon. Classic Universe move."

The group chuckles, amused yet intrigued.

Melanie laughs softly. "Messy but meaningful."

"Exactly," Bird Poop Lady says, giggling. "Standing there on the sidewalk, staring at this bird-bomb on my arm, it hit me. Cupcakes are my thing. They always have been. I've made them forever—for birthdays, weddings, baby showers, or just because. It's what I love doing, but I never imagined turning it into anything real."

Resa nods thoughtfully, voice calm. "Maybe life knew you needed a nudge you couldn't miss."

Bird Poop Lady smiles wider, warmth radiating from her. "That's how it felt—like permission. Not a sign telling me what to do. But a yes. A yes I didn't even know I'd been waiting for."

That's it. *Permission.* The words come back to me; *Courage chooses to move.* Maybe that's what a sign is. A yes, you didn't know you'd been waiting for, that gives you the courage to move.

Deni leans in. "And then what happened?"

Bird Poop Lady claps her hands together, her excitement impossible not to feel. "Everything happened! The moment I decided to do it, to open a cupcake shop, every step just appeared. A friend mentioned a tiny storefront space that was super affordable, just big enough to sell cupcakes. I got the keys almost immediately. I bake at home, bring everything fresh each morning, and I swear, from the day I opened two weeks ago, I've sold out every single afternoon."

A few women let out wows, one woman presses a hand to her chest, another breathes out, "That's beautiful."

"I've always dreamed of having a little bakery, a place to share my cupcakes," she says. "But it always felt impossible, so I kept it a hobby. Then the moment I said yes, life just... lined up. Every conversation led me to the next step. And every worry I had started to melt away the second I took that first step."

Fia lets out a happy sigh. "The bird poop prophecy," she says, grinning. "See? The universe doesn't need your plan. It just needs your yes."

Gentle laughter fills the space again, warm and affirming.

Maybe signs are invitations. Not direction, exactly, but permission to trust the subtle nudges already inside us.

Bird Poop Lady eagerly describes the cozy shop, colorful cupcakes, and quirky regulars who bring life to the bakery every day. Her joy is infectious, warming the circle with possibility and hope. She settles back into her chair, eyes sparkling. "Anyway, turns out even bird poop can be magical if you pay attention."

Deni wrinkles her nose playfully. "Girl, that's grace. If poop hit my sleeve, cupcake or not, I'd be chasing that bird with a shoe."

We laugh again, and a comforting silence settles over us.

Deni shifts in her seat, then blurts it out before she can second-guess herself. "Okay. I'm leaving Eric."

The room stills. I want to jump in and say, *yes, go, leave*—but I hold it. The room holds it. No gasps. No scrambling to fix. Just quiet, steady presence.

She nods once, like she's convincing herself. "Yep. Leaving him. Done." Then adds, almost immediately, "Or... I want to. I wanna leave him." Her voice falters, just enough to let the truth slip through. "Let's just say... watching your man flirt with a walking spray tan in front of your friends doesn't exactly scream soul mate."

No one laughs, but no one looks away either.

She shrugs, not looking up. "I know. I've said it before. But I'm tired. And it's gettin' harder to pretend it's fine when it's not."

Nobody rushes in. Nobody interrupts. Everyone listens intently, offering nods of recognition.

Fia finally breaks it, tilting her head. "So, wait—are we talkin' might leave, or already Googled moving boxes?"

Deni huffs a laugh, wiping under one eye with the side of her finger. "We're talkin' stared at my suitcase for twenty minutes and then ordered tacos instead."

The group exhales gently—some smiling, some misty-eyed.

Resa's voice is low and calm. "You don't have to leave to begin. Sometimes the beginning is just telling the truth. You don't need certainty, just the courage to stop pretending."

Deni nods quickly, like she wants to move past it, eyes still shiny. "I'm not sure what I'm doing yet. But thanks, Resa."

Fia squints into her tea. "He's like glitter in carpet—looks fun till you're stuck cleaning it up for the rest of your life."

Deni snorts.

Fia nods. "Just sayin' some sparkles aren't worth the mess."

Deni squeezes her hand, wiping a tear quickly. "Thanks."

Eventually, Deni lifts her head and glances around the circle. "Okay, who's next?" Her tone is lighter, warmth returning.

The circle goes quiet, expectant.

I smile. My next words feel big.

"I wrote a book." Hearing them out loud almost surprises me. "I didn't mean to, but it happened. And someone thinks it's worth publishing."

Resa rests her hand lightly over mine. "Yes," she says. "Someone does."

Murmurs of excitement fill the circle.

"And the weirdest thing?" I say. "Even though I titled it, *Signs*, it's not about signs—not the way I thought. It's about trusting yourself instead of looking outside for the answers. And when you do—when you choose yourself, and believe the knowing that's already in you, life sends little winks to let you know that you're not doing it alone."

Resa gives a small, knowing nod. "That's the shift— when you stop searching and start allowing, life can finally get through."

Fia lights up. "See? "You stop forcing it, and suddenly the universe gets a word in. Birds. Books. Breakthroughs. Boom."

Laughter breaks the moment. Each woman takes a turn—some talking, some just listening. Some stories are messy, some funny, some barely spoken aloud.

We stay like that until the night settles in around us— comfortable, unpolished, real.

As I head for the door, Deni pulls me into a quick hug. "Hey, thanks for coming. You belong here. There's just something about you that feels safe. It's weird, but a good weird."

"I'm glad I came," I say, not sure what it means to feel *safe* to someone, but the word *belong* stays with me.

I want to tell her, *Don't wait for love to stop hurting before you leave*. The words rise, ready. But I hold back. Deni must find her own way. I can't do it for her.

I give her hand a gentle squeeze, then let go and step toward the door.

18

A New Place, A New Voice

"Home arrives when nothing stands between you and yourself."

-Reid

TONIGHT FEELS OVERDUE. It's been a couple of months since I've seen Michael—him traveling with his girlfriend, me buried in book things.

His front door is open. "I brought wine," I call out, stepping inside.

He looks out from the kitchen. "Even better, you brought conversation." He waves me in and takes the bottle from my hand, inspecting the label. "Ah. A Bordeaux blend. Confident, generous, maybe a little misunderstood."

"The wine or your guest?"

He gives a half smile. "That's for the pairing to reveal."

I settle at the kitchen counter while he pours. The clink of glass and the velvety glug feel like coming home. Maybe this is what visiting my mom as an adult would've felt like—if life had allowed it.

Michael sits across from me, wine in hand, and studies me for a moment.

"You seem… different," he says. "Rooted."

"I am. This town—this life I'm building—it's what I didn't know I was missing. A real home."

"You stopped trying to fit in and ended up where you belong." He smiles. "How is the new place?"

"It's good. Really good," I say. "Every morning, I take my coffee to the porch and look out at the harbor. There's this one sailboat, the way it bobs with the tide reminds me to relax, let life carry me. I like that."

He listens with that calm presence I've come to know.

"I've got herbs growing in the kitchen window—basil, and the rosemary you gave me. Been making those simple recipes you wrote down. The roasted tomato one? Turns out I can cook. Sort of."

He grins, both proud and amused.

"And I can walk to Coffee Compass, to your house, to almost everything I care about. It's the first time I've ever felt like my life and my body were in the same place."

He holds my gaze for a moment. "You're home."

We sit with the quiet, the faint tick of the clock keeping time with the moment.

"You were right about Mystic," I say. "It's more than a town; it holds you while you find your way back to yourself."

"I wasn't sure it would be that for you," he says. "But I hoped."

I watch the red wine cling to the sides of my glass. "I thought belonging meant becoming what someone else wanted."

"What changed?"

I take a breath. "I stopped asking if I was allowed. I just… stayed. Let people in. Let them see me."

He nods slowly.

"I used to think I had to be special, or useful, or easy enough, for someone to care. But here—with you, with the women—I don't have to prove anything. Just show up."

Michael tilts his head. "That's the only thing love ever asks. That you let it see you."

"That's good. You should write that down."

He grins, playful. "Already did. Page 42 of my new book, *Nine Holes.*"

I chuckle. "Of course you did." I exhale slowly. "I miss our wine and movie nights."

"They're not exclusive to crisis," he says. "You can still come by. No heartbreak required."

"Good. Because I have a soft spot for metaphors in liquid form."

Michael laughs, then stands and grabs a second bottle. "Then tonight, a Sancerre. Light, but grounded. Refined, but doesn't perform. It just is."

"Sounds like someone I know."

He shrugs. "If the cork fits."

We carry our glasses to the porch and ease into the chairs. I reach into my bag and pull out a single copy—cream cover, soft matte finish, my name printed on the front like it belongs there.

"I brought you something," I say, holding it out.

Michael takes the book carefully. His fingers rest on the title, *Signs*.

"You did it."

"I did. I wanted you to have the first one."

He turns it over in his hands, then looks up. "I'm honored. Honestly." His eyes meet mine. "You've always had the words, Anelie. Now the world gets to read them." He opens to the first page.

"There's a dedication," I say, before he can flip past it.

His eyes move across the words: *To Michael, who offered sanctuary without needing a reason, and kindness without expectation.* He exhales slowly, still staring at the page.

His eyes fix on me. "You know, it's not only your life that changed. Mine did too. Having you here reminded me it's never too late to let love in. I'd given up on that. And now, for the first time in more than a decade, I'm with someone who makes me think about a life together."

I hold his gaze with a thank you that doesn't need words.

He closes the book, his thumb still resting on the inside cover. "I look forward to reading it."

We sip in silence for a few moments.

"Will you sign it for me?"

I blink, caught off guard. "Really?"

"Of course. I'd like my copy signed by the author." He sets the book in front of me and slides a pen over.

I write: *Michael, Thank you ... for everything. With love, Anelie*

He holds the book a moment, with both hands, before setting it carefully beside him.

"I have something for you, too," he says, then disappears inside and returns with a bottle. He sets it on the table between us. "For your new place."

I study the label, my eyes lingering on the vintage.

He follows my gaze. "That's the year she left."

I study his face. I know who he means.

"That year felt like losing everything," he says. "But the ending gave me space to return to what I loved—writing, wine, all the parts of me I'd buried to be what I thought she needed. And to find new things I loved: sharing meals, sharing space. It taught me that sometimes losing the life you thought was yours is the only way to find the one that truly is."

My fingertips trace the year on the label. "My mom died that year," I murmur.

"I didn't realize that was your year, too." A flicker of tenderness crosses his face. "Maybe that's why this bottle waited for tonight."

A silence passes between us—not heavy, just full. Shared grief, different shapes.

"So, why did you choose this bottle?" I ask.

"To remind you that what breaks us isn't always what ends us. Sometimes it's what frees us."

"When my mom died, it broke me. But it also…" I pause, the edges of the words catching in my throat. "… it was also a relief. Not because I wanted her gone, but because she'd already been leaving for years."

Michael gives a small nod of understanding.

"She'd been sick for a decade," I say. "It was slow, painful, undignified. And she was proud—fiercely independent—so losing control was its own kind of death. By the end, there was nothing left of her but pain. I think we were both ready. Letting go felt like mercy."

His voice is soft. "Endings are hard. But they're also beginnings, if you let them be."

"Leaving my ex, letting go of hoping things could be different, was the only way anything new could begin."

"Life waits until you're ready."

I nod. "It doesn't rush you. It waits with you… until you're ready to surrender and *begin again*."

He smiles at hearing his own words spoken back to him.

A breeze stirs the air around us, soft with salt and something that feels like confirmation.

"I mentioned your book to Eva, by the way. The bookstore owner."

My head tilts. "You did?"

He nods, casual. "She wants to host a signing, a little release party. She said your story gives people back to themselves."

"Wow."

"You should do it," he says with a wink. "I've been bragging about knowing the author, so some reputations are on the line."

I smile, exhale slowly, and take it in. A bookstore signing. For *my* book.

19

The Borrowed Gift

"What steadied your steps becomes another's courage to begin."

-Reid

EVA'S BOOKSHOP IS small. The floorboards creak, the air smells of dust and coffee. Books are stacked on antique tables, and a window nook waits with a cushion softened by the years. Handwritten staff picks jut out like flares: *Read this. Trust me.*

Eva waves from the back. "Our author is here!"

A small cluster of people already lingers near the front, browsing or waiting. Eva meets me halfway with a hug. "Nervous?"

"Oddly, no," I say. "It feels... good."

"Of course it does," she says. "You wrote something real. People can feel that."

Eva leads me to a table stacked high with *Signs*. A glass of water and a smooth gel pen sit waiting, a chalkboard propped beside them: *Book Signing Today – "Signs" – A Journey Back to Yourself.*

Resa walks in, wearing a green cardigan that matches her eyes, a smile already forming. "Well, there she is," she says.

I hug her. "You're the reason this happened."

"You're the reason it happened," she corrects gently. "I simply pointed toward what was already unfolding."

Behind her, Fia arrives in a blaze of scarves and bangles. "Behold, the mystical word weaver herself. You look like magic." She waves an imaginary wand, then says, "Sorry I'm late, I stopped to bless a dead squirrel. Long story."

I laugh. "Please tell me it wasn't a sign."

Fia winks. "You're lucky I didn't bring it. It had a vibe."

Deni slips in behind them, her eyes a little tired. "You did it," she says, hugging me tightly. "I'm so darn proud of you."

"You okay?" I ask softly.

She nods, then shrugs. "Today's not about me." And just like that, she offers a plate of chocolate-covered almonds to no one in particular.

The shop begins to fill with people. Women, mostly. A few men. Some I recognize from the spa. Their books already marked with sticky notes, or they buy one and cradle it like something fragile.

Eva speaks without a mic. "Some voices just belong. Anelie's is one of them. And her story feels like it was always meant to find its place here." She turns toward me. "Anelie, would you tell us why you wrote *Signs*?"

I step forward and take Eva's place. "I didn't set out to write a book, I was just trying to make sense of a moment that didn't make sense. I'd walked away from a relationship that shattered me, not in an obvious way, but in a thousand unacknowledged ways. Ways that slowly erase you until you feel like a stranger in your own life."

Around the room, heads nod.

"I kept asking for signs. Anything that would tell me what to do. But the signs didn't come—not the way I wanted. And eventually, I realized signs were never meant to give me answers. They were simply invitations to pay attention. Because the real direction wasn't out there."

A pause.

"It was here," I say, touching my chest. "It was me."

Eva's eyes shine. Fia makes a small sound that might be a sniffle. Resa watches like a proud parent. Michael, who I hadn't seen slip in, stands near the back with his arms folded across his chest, but the small smile tugging at the corner of his mouth says everything. Deni is off to the side, leaning against a display of new arrivals.

The line forms without instruction.

One by one, they come. Some speak. Some don't. Some press their book into my hands with shaky fingers. Some lean in and whisper, "Thank you."

A woman in her late forties, eyes rimmed in sleeplessness, waits until almost everyone else has gone. She's holding my book like it might disintegrate.

She reaches the table and sits across from me. "I read it twice." She doesn't look directly at me. "The first time, I cried. The second time, I made a plan."

I give her a look, an invitation to keep going.

"I'm leaving next week," she says. "I've been waiting for something to tell me it's okay. And reading your book... Well, it didn't give me permission, it reminded me I already had it."

Grief and gratitude swell in my chest; grief for her struggle, gratitude that my words could offer a way through.

I reach into my bag, pull out the compass and hold it between us. "I want you to have this."

Her eyes widen. "I can't—"

"It was meant to be passed on," I say.

She takes it like it's something holy. Her eyes glisten. She lowers the compass into her bag and presses her hand over mine.

"Thank you," she says.

I smile, handing back her copy of the book. "I'm glad they both found you."

She nods once and leaves. A woman carrying herself forward.

Across the room, Resa catches my eye and gives a single, slow nod.

Michael walks over after the last book is signed. "You've come a long way since that first night over a bottle of Viognier and unlearning old patterns." He winks. "Now you're the one handing out compasses."

I smile. "Don't worry—I still have no idea where I'm going."

And I don't. But that was never the point.

.

20

The Life That Found Me

*"What is meant for you does not come by force,
but by surrender."*

-Reid

IT'S BEEN THREE months since the book signing. I glance around the kitchen of my little guest cottage. Michael's gift is still alive despite my lack of a green thumb—rosemary stretching toward the sun. Morning light falls on the cards and quotes taped to the fridge and the gallery postcard catches my eye. I lean against the counter, flip it over and read what I scribbled nearly a year ago: *No more proving I belong. I am the weather. I arrive.*

Back then, I wrote it as a declaration I barely believed, reflecting more hope than truth. Now, I feel its weight. I don't need permission to exist. I belong, here, in a life that unfolded when I stopped forcing one. Not despite who I am. Because of it.

I trace the edge of the card. *I am the weather*—ever-changing, uncontainable by design. *I arrive*—not for approval, but because I was always meant to. Exactly as I am.

Outside, the familiar sailboat drifts, anchored yet not still.

The living room is barely a corner, but it holds enough: a soft chair that hugs back, a tiny bookshelf, and my desk—a small wooden table by the window overlooking the harbor. Above it hangs Fia's gift, a watercolor feather, suspended mid-fall, framed in driftwood. A notecard in her loopy handwriting is tucked into the frame:

You are exactly where you're supposed to be.

I am.

The open patio door carries in the sound of water and seagulls. And the peace of nothing needing to be different.

The day begins. At the top of my inbox, a subject line stops me: *Congratulations!* My finger hovers, unsteady. I click, and stare: *Signs is a New York Times Bestseller.*

The message from my publisher is brief, just a few lines confirming that *Signs* has debuted at number twelve on the nonfiction list. A link. A screenshot. My name.

My breath leaves me in one long, soundless exhale. I don't call anyone. I just sit.

And cry.

This wasn't something I forced. I didn't chase it. I just told the truth.

I think back to the woman I was when I arrived in Mystic—tired, unrooted, holding a compass with no needle, asking the sky for a sign. Turns out, the sign wasn't outside me. It was this. This moment. This cottage. This harbor. This life. A book I wrote for myself, and maybe, in some roundabout way, for anyone who ever needed a sign that the real answer was always there, waiting. That trusting yourself isn't just okay—it's necessary.

I smile, small, real. This wasn't the dream I chased. It's the life that unfolded when I stopped chasing. One just for me.

I don't tell anyone right away—not Michael, not the readers who follow me, not even Deni, who will absolutely scream.

I head for Coffee Compass. Resa's the one who told me it mattered. Who said, let me show someone. She never needed proof—but here it is. Proof that what she saw in my words is being felt by others.

Resa is behind the counter, speaking in that gentle tone she reserves for conversations that matter. She's mid-laugh, hand resting on the arm of a man facing away from me—tall, silver-haired, a leather pack slung across his shoulder.

He turns as I reach the counter. Our eyes lock, and the moment fractures open, stilling everything around it. The hum of the cafe fades. For a breath, it's only us. I don't know him, but every part of me insists I do.

He gives a nod, enough to hold me there.

"I'm Reid," he says, offering his hand.

Something stirs in my chest. The name. The presence. The handwriting I've been seeing for months on the chalkboard behind him. My eyes find the board.

What if the dream didn't come true,
because something better was on its way? -Reid

I look back at him. Of course. *That* Reid.

"Anelie," I say, taking his hand. His grip is steady, grounding. His eyes hold me as if he feels it too.

He smiles. "Good to meet you."

"You, too," I whisper.

He nods to Resa, then turns back to me, his eyes lingering. He smiles again and moves toward the exit. A moment later, the door swings shut behind him. The air feels changed, charged as if something important arrived, then slipped away before I could name it.

I stand, motionless.

Resa watches the door close. "Well," she says, not looking at me, "that was inevitable."

I blink. "What was?"

"Things that you don't see coming but were always on their way."

Before I can decipher what she means, she asks, smiling, "Coffee with cream?"

"Yes, please."

I glance at the chalkboard. The question. The now-empty doorway. As she hands me my drink, I hear, "Did you just meet Reid?"

Fia appears from the hallway, holding a muffin like a sacred object. "You met Reid, didn't you? I saw it. That pause. That pause was everything."

"I guess I did," I say, still catching up to myself.

Fia gasps. "That's like... spiritual bingo. You just filled a row."

I let her words hang for a second, then draw a breath, clearing the haze. "I've got news."

Both heads turn. Fia practically vibrates. "Tell us everything."

I exhale slowly. "*Signs*... made the *New York Times* bestseller list."

Resa looks up, her eyes warm and clear. "Of course it did."

Fia shrieks, muffled only by the muffin she's trying not to choke on. "Shut. Up. You're famous."

I laugh. "Hardly."

Resa leans forward slightly. "Not famous, Anelie. Found... by the people who needed it."

Her words reach deeper than congratulations.

Fia sets the muffin down. "I knew it. I felt it in my wrist bones."

They both watch me for a moment, not saying anything more. And I realize... this is it. The reward isn't the list or the label. It's this: that what I wrote, trying to make sense of my own story, is helping others make sense of theirs.

I carry the mug to my corner by the window.

21

No Map Required

"What belongs to you stands beyond your dreams, waiting only for you."

-Reid

MICHAEL REACHES MY door as I'm opening it, a bottle of wine in one hand, and a gift bag in the other.

"You're early," I say, smiling.

He lifts the bottle. "Couldn't risk you ruining my recipe with a substitute wine."

I laugh. "Puh-leese, like I'd dare."

He scans the kitchen and rests his eyes on the rosemary plant. "This place suits you."

"Thanks." It does.

The table is already set on the patio. I bring out a serving bowl with the pasta—his recipe, heavy on the olive oil and citrus—and he opens the wine.

We eat slowly, the way Michael always does—tasting, not just consuming. Conversation flows naturally—a few book-signing stories, a golf club moment that made him laugh, his recent travel to France with his love, my latest note from a reader who said it felt like I was sitting beside her, giving words to the struggle she's carried for years.

I look out at the water. I've let others tell me where to go, how to love, what success looked like. In doing that, I silenced the small voice inside me that always knew the way.

"I don't think I ever let myself imagine a life of my own," I say. "I kept following other people's maps, hoping they'd lead somewhere that felt like home." I twirl the pasta, citrus rising from the steam.

Michael's gaze lingers on the harbor a moment. "The path makes a lot more sense when it's your own."

"For the first time in my life, I feel like I'm home," I say. "I never knew to imagine it. Not a person or a place. Home is where you stop searching. Not walls, not a view. Home is when nothing in you wants to leave."

"Life rarely gives us what we think we want," he says. "It usually gives us what we need. And sometimes, it gives us something better than we even knew to ask for."

I smile at him. "It does, doesn't it."

Above us, twinkle lights hang like stars waiting to be wished on, the night settling around everything.

"I thought being strong meant it was all on me—to figure it out, to hold everything together, force it to mean something," I say. "But looking back, I see how life kept showing up. In signs. In people. In moments I didn't recognize then. I was never alone."

Michael tilts his head, thoughtful. "Sometimes that's all we need, isn't it? Just to feel less alone in the not knowing."

A gentleness opens in me. It all belonged. None of it was wasted. I wasn't off course. Every turn I thought was wrong was part of what carried me here. We all move at our own pace. Deni left Eric, but she's still holding on. Not because she doesn't see the truth, she's just still hoping for a different ending. She's not behind. She's just not done yet. There was a time I would've tried to save her—push, convince, show her what she couldn't, or wouldn't, admit. But that's not love. That was me refusing to accept she had to find her own way. Believing that if she followed my path, she could skip the pain.

Now, I let her be where she is. Everyone gets there in their own time. And sometimes what looks like the wrong path is the one that builds the strength for different choices next time.

"I used to think loving someone meant showing them the way out." I give a small smile that says I see it now—what he did for me. "Now I think it's just standing beside them... until they're ready."

"Sometimes the most generous thing we can do," he says, a glint in his eye, "is shut up and pass the wine."

I laugh. "Exactly. Caring without controlling."

"Exactly." He nods, looks out at the harbor, then back at me. "Can I tell you what I see?"

"Always."

"You came here looking like you'd been holding your breath for years, waiting for the next disappointment. Now there's an ease in you, like you're done proving yourself."

I take a breath. "It's true."

"You've stopped trying to earn a place in rooms where you never belonged, trying to be who you were never meant to be. And that's how the life meant for you finally found you."

"You're right. And I still can't believe it sometimes."

"And now you've written a book that's helping people," he says. "Not by pointing the way, but by showing there is one."

We sit in the hush that follows. Everything that matters already is.

After Michael has gone, I clean up, pour the last inch of wine, and settle into the chair by the window. The harbor is dark now, only the soft sway of mast lights visible in the distance.

On the table beside me, a notecard peeks out from a book, catching my attention. I slide it free.

No map required. Fia tucked it into my hand months ago at the *Signs* event. I used it as a bookmark, kept it without knowing why.

I used to think a little plastic compass was guiding me. Same with the signs. But they were never meant to guide anything. They weren't directions, they were pauses—invitations to listen, nudges to pay attention, reminders that we're never alone, confirmations that we're exactly where we're supposed to be.

Fia's voice echoes: *Life throws feathers, not blueprints.*

I smile, not because I know where I'm going, but because I've stopped needing to.

I was never lost. Just tired of the map.

Author Note

Signs

"The universe is written in the language of signs."
                                                    - Paulo Coelho

I wasn't planning to write an author's note, but while I was writing *I Thought It Was a Sign,* signs started showing up— small, uncanny winks from Life itself, too perfectly timed to ignore.

I spend most of my writing time in coffee shops, so it's not surprising that the first wink came while I was waiting for coffee.

At Nambah Coffee in La Verne, California, I was in line to order when curiosity (and my obsession with words) nudged me, so I looked up *Nambah.* From the island of Java—fitting. It means *improve.* I grinned. Of course it does. I had finished writing this book and was working on improving it. A small thing, but it landed with that hum of alignment that says, pay attention. Then, when I asked for the Wi-Fi password, I laughed out loud: **perfecttiming.**

It was as if Life leaned across the counter and whispered, *See? I'm paying attention too.*

Another day, another coffee shop—Classic Coffee in Glendora, California. I was working on a scene about how we're exactly where we're supposed to be and had just written a new line: *You are exactly where you are supposed to be, until it's time to be somewhere else.*

When I left, there it was on the reader board I'd somehow missed on my way in: *You are exactly where you need to be.*

And then there was the painting. I'd been writing the scene about an art piece called *Becoming Weather*—an image that came to me out of nowhere: a swirl of sky meeting sea, alive but calm. Later that week, I walked into a hotel bathroom (of all places) and froze. Hanging on the wall was the painting I had imagined. The same colors. The same motion. I just stood there and laughed—again.

Signs like that showed up the entire time I wrote this book. Not big, flashing arrows—just small nods, winks, perfectly timed whispers saying, *Keep going. You're exactly where you need to be.*

Maybe that's what "signs" really are—not predictions or guarantees, but quiet confirmations that the story we're living is unfolding in sync with something larger. Something that sees us, nudges us, and occasionally uses a Wi-Fi password to remind us that the timing really is perfect.

※

If this story found you when you needed it, I'd be grateful for a short review. It helps the book find its next reader at the right moment, too.

Thanks!

About The Author

Dayna Mason (also writing as Dayna Reid) is an award-winning author, columnist, podcaster, and minister. She has written several bestselling books on weddings, funerals, love, and personal growth, as well as a children's book—and now makes her debut in fiction. Born and raised in Seattle, she now resides in Southern California.

Find her on Instagram: @DaynaJoAuthor